THAT SNOWY NIGHT

My life is about to become a holiday cliché.

Delilah

I never think I'll see Alex Blake again. Most certainly not on the side of a snowy Alaskan highway.

Alex is a hazy memory—stolen summer kisses that keep me warm on lonely nights.

Life and geography got in the way. When my car skids off the highway in the darkness in Alaska, I'm plenty bitter and I've lost all faith in fantasies.

I didn't count on Alex, didn't count on his kisses setting me on fire, and most certainly not on him betting it all on us.

Alex

I never could forget Delilah Carter. She was my fantasy, but I figured that's all she'd ever be.

Until I find her stranded on a snowy highway a few thousand miles away from where I last saw her. She's still my fantasy.

But, this time, I get to make it all come true.

Chapter One

DELILAH

"I've got this," I said to absolutely no one.

Unless I was counting my rental car and my hastily packed bag sitting in the back seat behind me. Snow was falling steadily outside, and it was already dark. The early darkness was a minor detail I hadn't considered when I scheduled my flight.

December in Alaska meant the sun made its bow pretty freaking early. It was a bit different from North Carolina in that regard.

"I can totally do this," I said, trying to inject a hint of confidence into my voice.

A few minutes later, all my internal cheering felt useless when my compact SUV rental hit a patch of ice and skidded down a small embankment off the side of the road.

"Fuck! There's probably a bear here."

Maybe I was talking to myself a bit much, but it was a habit. Despite my stated worry about a bear, I was strangely not too shaken. Not just yet.

I eyed the clock on the dashboard. It wasn't even five in the evening, and it was almost fully dark. Scarcity didn't capture the state of traffic here. I hadn't seen more than ten cars since I'd driven beyond the outskirts of Anchorage, a full hour and a half behind me, and my destination, Diamond Creek, was another few hours ahead. My normal can-do attitude wasn't too helpful this far from home, and a wave of anxiety crested inside me.

Fighting against it—because I was *not* that kind of girl—I took several deep breaths. I was tough. I could totally handle this. Hell, I threw out drunk men over six feet tall on a weekly basis at the bar where I worked, so surely, I could call for help and potentially even get myself out of this little ditch.

Climbing out, I surveyed the situation with nothing more than the headlights to help me out. Okay, ditch didn't exactly capture where my rental had landed. The side of the highway dropped off steeply beyond the edge of the road. There wasn't much of a shoulder at all.

Fortunately, I was only a few feet off the road, but the incline was steep enough I certainly wouldn't be shoving this car back onto the road by myself.

"Fuck!"

The wind blew my curse away, not even leaving an echo behind. The snow was blowing around, swirling in the darkness. For a woman who liked to think she was usually prepared and smart, I felt woefully unprepared and astonishingly stupid.

Winter in Alaska was a far cry from the winters in the Blue Ridge Mountains where I came from. Oh, we got snow there, and we had plenty of winding, twisty mountain roads that got icy in the blink of an eye on a cold winter night. But it certainly didn't get dark this early, and even the more rural areas had more traffic than this.

A gust of wind buffeted me, and the cold snow stung my cheeks. With a sigh, I trudged around to the driver's side of the SUV and climbed in. When the door shut, muting the sound of the wind and blowing snow, my relief was overwhelming.

Except for one small problem. I was alone on the side of a dark highway in Alaska, and it was freezing cold outside.

Christmas was a mere week away. I just hoped I survived the night to see it. I didn't even want to contemplate the potential headlines if I froze to death in my little SUV. *Idiotic tourist who thought she could handle winter driving* would be a good start.

I burrowed into my down jacket and adjusted the angle in my seat so I could see any headlights approaching on the highway. After a solid twenty minutes without a single passing car, a humming sense of panic started to churn in my stomach. I couldn't exactly climb out and hike because I had nowhere to go here. As far as I knew, miles of highway stretched between towns in this area, and it was well below zero with the wind howling louder by the second.

On the heels of a gust of wind, which rattled the SUV, I saw two distinct beams of light illuminating the highway. *Thank you, Jesus.* I really should've prayed more than I did. I'd been raised better, but I'd slipped.

Just as I was debating whether I should climb out or hope they saw my headlights in the darkness, I saw those two friendly beams shine straight into the back of my vehicle as what appeared to be a truck came to a stop.

"Yes, yes, yes!" I chanted to myself.

Scrambling out, I looked up to see a tall man stepping down the incline off the side of the highway.

God, I hope he's not an ax murderer.

The gruff chuckle I heard through the wind cued me to the fact that my inside thought wasn't so inside. My thoughts just strolled out of my mouth sometimes.

"Sorry about that. Perils of being a woman and all," I explained as I stopped in front of the man and looked up.

My mouth nearly fell open when I got a good look. I *knew* this man.

"Alex Blake?"

"Delilah?"

"Oh, my God."

My heart leaped into a tumbling routine that would've done a gymnast proud. Holy shit.

"What are you doing here? Come on, let's get in my truck," Alex said without giving me time to answer.

While my mind was skidding sideways at this strange turn of events, a boy who I'd once had a wild crush on and was now very clearly *all* man reached for me as I got closer, curling his hand around my elbow.

"This is crazy," I murmured over the howl of the wind.

Alex's chuckle sent a shiver chasing down my spine. "Crazy is one way to put it," he replied, his voice barely audible as a bracing gust of wind hit us.

"Hang on, let me get my bag," I called over the wind.

Alex angled us toward the driver's side door of my rental SUV. I grabbed my purse from the front while he tugged my bag out of the back where I directed him to when he asked.

I simply followed along as Alex kept a firm grip on me with one hand and my bag with the other. I barely noticed the snow striking in stinging spikes against my cheeks as my mind stumbled at the shock of encountering this man.

My pulse had taken off like a rocket, and I was acutely aware of his easy strength as he basically towed me through the knee-deep snow. In short order, we were beside his truck, and he was opening the door.

I managed to almost fall just trying to climb in. With the road icy under my feet and being completely flustered, coordination wasn't my friend.

Alex, being the gentleman he was, or, rather the gentleman I recalled, helped me in and waited until I was fully seated before he closed the passenger door. I watched as he ducked his head to lean into the snow and rounded the front of his truck.

Another blast of wind followed him into the truck. Blessedly, the thud of the door closing muffled the sound and cut off the biting cold outside.

I held my hands in front of the heater vents and glanced over at Alex. The shock of seeing him provoked a visceral reaction from my body. My heart felt as if it had been jump-started, and my belly plummeted, falling and spinning as I stared into his rich brown gaze.

The last time I saw Alex Blake—a man I had never forgotten—had been at a summer camp in the mountains in Colorado. My presence there was almost as wildly unlikely as me encountering him here in Alaska. Alex had been oh, so handsome with dark amber hair and espresso eyes; a strong, square jaw; and a lean, rangy body.

I liked Alex *so, so* much back then. Crushes at summer camp were as close to a mirage as anything could be. He should've been nothing but a footnote in my life, yet I had *never* forgotten him. Looking at his mouth, strong and bold, I still recalled the feel of his lips moving over mine and the slow, sensual tease of his tongue.

"What the hell are you doing on the side of the road in Alaska a week before Christmas, Delilah?"

Chapter Two

ALEX

Delilah Carter eyed me carefully. "That's a good question," she finally said.

"I assume you have an answer," I countered.

Delilah bit the corner of her bottom lip—her tempting, plump lip with a dimple in the center.

"Well, it's kind of a fluke," she finally said.

I waited while she stared at me, her green eyes as stunning as I recalled. The lighting in my truck cab might've been low, but it was nearly impossible to dim Delilah's unique, striking beauty.

Uncertainty flickered in her eyes, and she took a deep breath. Letting it out with a gusty sigh, she finally broke away from my gaze as she leaned her head against the seat. "Crazy as it may sound, I'm here for an all-expense-paid ski vacation in Diamond Creek. An old friend gave it to me. It's a place called Last Frontier Lodge."

"Seriously?"

She rolled her head to the side, nodding. "Seriously," she replied, a tinge of pink cresting on her cheeks.

I felt my lips curling into a smile, shaking my head as I

absorbed the ramifications of our situation. "Well, I'll be damned. That's exactly where I'm going."

Delilah's eyes widened. "You're kidding."

I shook my head. "Definitely not."

As we sat there with the wind howling outside my truck and the sound of the snow striking the windshield, sparks filled the air as a humming electricity spun to life around us. It had been just a few kisses years ago.

Yet I'd never forgotten Delilah. I had wanted her so fiercely those hazy weeks one summer when we were both too young, but a memory was a tricky thing. Some things got blown up to cartoonish proportions, and others slid off into nothing. It was hard to trust and know what was accurate.

"I tried to find you," I said, my words surprising me.

Delilah angled toward me. I wanted to trace along the curve of her cheek and smooth her mussed dark hair, damp from the snow outside. Her brows hitched up at my comment, and her breath came out in a startled little puff.

Her teeth sank into her bottom lip again, nibbling it lightly and drawing my eyes to her mouth. Fuck me. She had a mouth made for sin with plump and inviting lips. I could even remember what she tasted like—sweet with a hint of vanilla.

"Oh," she said softly, her word catching slightly in her throat. She swallowed, the sound audible in the small space.

Before either of us spoke again, a truck passed by, sending a splash of icy slush against mine. The abrupt sound reminded me of where we were.

"We should get going. In this weather, it might take longer than usual to get there. We have at least two more hours of driving."

Delilah straightened in her seat. "Of course. You're sure you don't mind?"

"Giving you a ride?" I asked as I put my truck into gear.

"Yeah. I'm not sure what I'll do about that SUV. It's a rental."

"Well, it's safe where it is for now," I said as I slowly pulled off the side of the highway. "In case you didn't notice, there's not much traffic. It's far enough off the road that it should be fine. I suggest you call the rental place and leave a message. They can probably arrange for a tow truck from Anchorage to pick it up tomorrow. You can either get a rental in Diamond Creek, or I'll give you a ride back."

"If you don't mind, I'll call the rental company right now."

"Go right ahead," I replied as I slowly picked up speed.

Delilah made the quick call. As expected, they told her to leave the vehicle where it was, and they would arrange for a tow.

After she ended the call, only the sound of the heater blowing at full force filled the truck cab. I drove through the darkness, my body tight and a strange sense falling over me. I didn't know why Delilah's path had collided with mine again, but I intended to grab the chance with both hands.

———

A few hours later, I rolled to a stop in the parking lot at Last Frontier Lodge, a premier ski resort in Diamond Creek where the feet of the mountains kissed the shoreline of the ocean. For now, the darkness and blowing snow cloaked the spectacular view.

Glancing at Delilah, I said, "Here we are."

Delilah peered ahead through the windshield at the beckoning lights of the lodge. It was lit up with the ski slopes curving into the darkness and the lights glittering through the snow.

When she turned to me, and her smile stretched wider, my heart gave a funny little tumble. Just like before, Delilah had this strange effect on me, as if she tapped into a part of me only available to her. I recalled wanting to *really* get to know her that summer and how much we talked and teased.

I also recalled being a little mystified by how much I wanted her. But damn, every time I'd kissed her, I felt alive in a way I'd never experienced since.

A gust of wind rattled the windshield, nudging me out of my memories. "Let's go on in," I said.

She got a little prickly when I insisted on carrying her bag, but I ignored her. Though she gave off a sense of steely vulnerability, I wanted to know the woman underneath her sharp-edged exterior.

As I pushed through the heavy wooden front door into the lodge, the wind and snow blew in with us, the rushing sound muting once the door fell shut. The enveloping warmth was a relief from the icy temperature outside. Glancing around, I absorbed the space. I'd been to Last Frontier Lodge a number of times. It was an easy getaway for me from Willow Brook, and I had a few friends in Diamond Creek.

Although it was late, the lodge bustled with guests checking in at the reception desk, and the murmur of voices from the restaurant spilled through the archway beyond the reception area.

"There you are!"

I glanced around, my eyes landing on my twin sister standing over to one side with her husband, who also happened to be my best friend. Nate Fox had his arm slung around Holly's shoulders. Nate almost never had his hands off my sister. It had taken some getting used to, but I'd adjusted to their relationship and was happy for them. They'd gotten married just a few months ago.

"Hey, Holl," I called as I glanced back at Delilah. "That's my sister over there. Come on, let me introduce you."

One of Delilah's dark brows arched up. "Are you ...?"

She stopped her question when I shook my head. "It's my sister. Trust me, you're not gonna be able to avoid her."

Delilah looked uncertain, but she followed along when I began walking over to where Holly and Nate were waiting. I didn't miss Holly's curious gaze on Delilah as we approached.

"Alex," Holly said immediately, brushing her long blond hair off her shoulders. "You're late."

"Nice to see you too, Holl," I countered with a grin.

Nate chuckled, his brown eyes tipping up with his smile. "Holly thought you'd be here this afternoon."

"The roads are pretty sketchy," Holly said pointedly.

"I hit the road later than I planned, but I'm here safe and sound. Anyway, this is Delilah," I said, gesturing to Delilah, who was hanging back slightly.

My twin sister's sharp brown gaze shifted like a laser to Delilah. I could practically see her trying to X-ray the situation.

"Delilah's rental car ran off the road, so I picked her up and gave her a ride. Oddly enough, we met once before at that summer camp in Colorado," I explained.

Holly stepped forward. "Hi, I'm Holly," she said, offering her hand.

"Delilah, Delilah Carter," Delilah offered in return.

"What brings you here?" Holly asked. I considered clapping at her restraint. I knew my sister was about to burst with curiosity.

"I would imagine I'm here for the same reason you are," Delilah replied. "To ski."

Holly smiled slowly. "I guess that *is* obvious," she said after a moment.

Nate caught Delilah's eyes, casting her an easy smile. "Nice to meet you. Nate Fox."

"My fiancé," Holly chimed in.

"Oh, congratulations. When's the wedding?" Delilah asked.

Holly wrinkled her nose, giving a sheepish smile when Nate rolled his eyes. "She keeps forgetting I'm actually her husband now. We just got married a few months ago."

Holly poked him in the side with her elbow. "I don't

forget! It's just you were my fiancé longer than we've been married."

A cluster of guests filed past us, bumping into Delilah and effectively ending our brief conversation with Holly and Nate. "I should go check in. I'll be right back," she said.

Chapter Three

DELILAH

"Go ahead," Alex replied. "I called ahead when I left Willow Brook, so I'm already checked in. I'm assuming you guys are too?" He glanced at Holly and Nate.

"Of course. We were waiting for you so we can get dinner together. Why don't you join us for dinner after you check in?" Holly suggested, looking at me.

Seeing as I knew absolutely no one here, other than Alex and now them, I had no easy way to refuse. Not that I wanted to. "That would be nice. Let me check in so I can drop off my bag and freshen up."

"I'm going to go check out my room," Alex said, just as I started to turn away. "How about we all meet back here in about fifteen minutes?"

"Sure," I replied before heading over to the line at the reception desk.

A cluster of guests hummed around me, but I barely noticed. My mind was still reeling over running into Alex like this.

The nearly electric force of his presence had sharpened the edges of my memories of him. Although my attraction to him had been unsettling in its power before, I had forgotten how easy it was to be around him. He was funny, charming, and gracious. He exuded a confident masculinity. It didn't hurt that he was so freaking handsome with his dark blond hair and espresso eyes.

When I got to the front of the line, a woman with auburn hair and jade eyes smiled over at me. "Hi there, how are you this evening?"

"Considering I skidded off the highway on the way here from Anchorage, I'm doing quite all right," I replied with a wry laugh.

"Oh, no! Are you okay? How did you get here?" Her questions came in rapid succession. "I'm Marley, by the way."

"Nice to meet you. I'm Delilah Carter. I was lucky enough that another guest on the way here stopped to check on me and gave me a ride. Conveniently, he wasn't a stranger. I'm feeling a bit like I'm in a movie. I still can't believe I ran into someone I know on the side of a snowy highway all the way across the country from where I live."

Marley grinned. "That's wild. If you don't mind me asking, who gave you a ride?"

"Alex Blake. Do you know him?"

"Oh, Alex. Of course I know him! He comes down here pretty often for weekend ski trips with friends and also does mechanic work at the airport every so often."

"So I learned," I returned with a smile. During the remainder of our drive, Alex and I had caught up with each other, so I had a sketch of his life.

"Well, let me look up your room," Marley said, glancing down. "What name is the reservation under again?"

"Mine. Delilah Carter. It was originally under Remy Martin," I explained, referring to an old friend who moved from North Carolina to Alaska. "They had a change of plans."

Marley clicked on the keyboard, and I could see her hand moving the mouse to scroll. When the moment stretched on, my gut churned. As her eyes met mine again, she looked concerned, her brow furrowing and her mouth twisting to the side.

"I'm sorry, we don't seem to have a reservation for you. I found the record, but it looks like it was accidentally canceled instead of replacing Remy's name with yours. There's a notation with your name, and there's no refund listed, so I absolutely know it's our mistake. The problem is we're booked solid. I am so, *so* sorry," Marley explained.

My chest felt tight, and tears pressed hot at the backs of my eyes. I'd been trying to keep it together for too long, and it had just been *that* kind of day and *that* kind of year. It was a fitting end for everything, a dollop of one more thing going wrong on top of my train wreck of a year.

Marley clearly sensed my distress even though I hadn't said a word.

"Obviously, we will offer you another stay at no charge," she said quickly. "Unfortunately, I'll have to see if we can find another place for you because we are at capacity."

I swallowed, ignoring the tears stinging my eyes. "Um, okay, that would be great."

Right then, Alex materialized at my side. "All checked in?" he asked.

I truly craved the power to go up in smoke and remove myself from this situation. I wasn't up for rolling with the punches at this moment. I'd had an over twelve-hour flight to get here and managed to keep my spirits up even when I skidded off the road. I couldn't seem to scramble up my composure, but I tried.

"Um, not really. Seems like my reservation got messed up. Marley, here, is going to find me somewhere else to stay," I explained with a tight smile.

Alex sensed my obvious distress because his arm slid around my shoulders as he leaned over to ask Marley something. I prayed I wasn't going to burst into tears in front of him, Marley, and the people milling about the reception area.

My eyes bounced around, taking in the holiday decorations. Evergreen wreaths were hung in a few places with cheerful holiday lights strung along the ceiling and winding around the doorways.

My brain cued in finally, and I picked up on the thread of Alex and Marley's conversation. "I promise, Alex. I will find her somewhere else to stay, and she'll get two free weeks here whenever she wants. The only problem is we're totally booked at the moment. There simply isn't anywhere for me to put her."

"You can share my room," Alex said firmly.

"Are you ...?" I stopped talking when he shook his head.

"If you're about to ask me if I'm sure, of course I'm sure. You're here for a ski vacation, so you'll have one. What Marley probably doesn't want to tell you just yet is that the likelihood of her finding another place for you to stay this time of year is slim to none."

Marley grimaced. "Alex, you never know."

"It's a good bet you won't. Almost everything is closed as far as hotels except for you." His eyes shifted to me again. "I'll sleep on the pullout couch. The bed is all yours. You're here for a vacation, so you should have one. Even if Marley finds you a place, this is the only ski lodge around. It's a great place to be over the holidays."

As I stood there staring at Alex, I didn't know what to say. What I wanted was my own room for the escape I had sought in coming here. With that slipping out of my grasp, I didn't want to be floundering to find another place.

Breaking from Alex's gaze, I looked over at Marley. "Tell me seriously. What are my chances of finding another place?"

Marley sighed. "Not great," she said with a frown. "I promise we'll get you a free week here. You pick the time, and we'll make it happen. I'm really, *really* sorry about this.

Honestly, I'd offer to let you stay in our private quarters, but we have family visiting for the holidays, so there's no extra space anywhere."

Calling on my depleted reserves of sanity, I took a deep breath and nodded at her before looking back at Alex. "If you're sure you don't mind, let's bunk together. I'll pay—" I began.

Alex shook his head. "You're not paying for anything. The room's already covered." He didn't wait for my reply. "Come on then." He steered me firmly away from the reception desk. It was only then I noticed the line of people stacking up behind me.

I wanted to curl up into Alex's warmth and strength, which made no sense. For God's sake, I barely knew him. A heady two weeks of crushing on him that culminated in a few crazy hot kisses when we were teenagers almost fifteen years ago didn't translate to knowing him well. I took a deep breath and tried to shake some sanity into my brain as he steered us through the crowded reception area and down a side hallway where we stopped in front of a bank of elevators.

I looked up at him, intending to thank him, but the doors swished open, and a cluster of people spilled out, filling the space with voices and laughter. We filed into the empty elevator, and quiet descended when the doors shut behind us. Alex tapped a button for the third floor.

The moment I looked into his dark gaze, my heart did a little flip, and my belly spun. In this tiny, enclosed space, my body fizzled with awareness. My mind flashed to those kisses so many years ago when I was younger. Even then, I had been cynical. But oh, I hadn't forgotten how those kisses felt. Most definitely not.

The air filled with sparks. I distantly wondered if I was crazy. It was dawning on me that it might be a challenge to share a room with Alex for a week.

Chapter Four

ALEX

Delilah stood beside me in the elevator. Her green eyes were dark, and her cheeks slightly flushed. Seeing that the distress had faded from her gaze gave me relief. Although I couldn't say I knew her well even though the feel of her mouth was permanently burned into my brain, I sensed she was not a woman who accepted help easily. Even when our paths had crossed all those years ago, she had exuded a sense of fierce independence.

I hadn't offered to share my room merely to grab the chance I never got the last time we met. Yet I was wondering if that wasn't such a bad idea.

Delilah stared at me, her tongue darting out and moistening her lower lip. I took in the delicate arch of her brows, the clean lines of her face, and the determined set of her jaw. My eyes dropped down, noticing the rapid flutter of her pulse in her neck.

Although a corner of my mind was telling me, rather sternly, not to kiss her and that I should be a gentleman, I moved on instinct.

As if her body was prey to the same magnetic force

humming around us, Delilah stepped in my direction just as I moved toward her. Her scent—which had driven me nearly insane after I picked her up on the side of the snowy road—drifted up to me. She was sweet, sultry, and so damn sexy she made my knees weak.

I held the handle of her bag in one hand. I let go because I needed both hands for this. Brushing her hair away from her face, I let the fingers of one hand slide into her silky locks as I cupped her nape. I slid my other palm down her spine, satisfaction rolling through me at the soft hitch in her breath.

"What are the chances we'd meet again like this?" I asked.

Her eyes darkened, her mouth curling at one corner as she shrugged. I sensed she wasn't one to give away smiles easily, so I felt as if I'd won something.

"I don't know. I'm wondering the same thing myself."

"I need to test a theory."

"A theory?" One dark brow arched high.

"Well, maybe a memory. I'm pretty sure that last kiss we shared was the best kiss of my life, so I need to double-check."

Delilah's cheeks flushed a deeper shade of pink, and her smile stretched to the other corner of her mouth. "Okay. Go right ahead."

When I stepped closer to her and heard the catch in her breath, desire bolted through me. I didn't know what the hell I was doing here with Delilah. Yet I'd never been able to shake thoughts about what might have been with us.

There had been no glorious heartbreak and no ugly breakup. We had simply gone our separate ways after those hazy summer days. I'd never forgotten her, though. Every so often, I'd wonder where she was and how she was doing. Each time I thought of her, I figured I'd always be left with nothing but my memories.

Yet here she was.

Shifting closer, I could feel the heat emanating from her. Her scent—one I hadn't even known I remembered—spun around me like smoke, sweet and spicy with an edge to it. Just like Delilah. My thoughts and my usual sense of control were slipping.

I tightened my grip on the reins, struggling to check the lust coursing through me. It was rushing with a force I couldn't ignore. "So tell me, Delilah," I murmured. "Did you ever wonder what might happen?"

Her breasts pressed against my chest when she took another breath, her flashing green eyes holding mine. The girl I remembered had a prickly exterior. She still did, but it was even more sharpened by the years. I sensed she didn't want to answer my question, but she didn't back down.

"Maybe," she replied, her tone husky.

"I definitely did."

I was pushing her, and I didn't know why. The random chance of our encounter galvanized me. The chance of finding her on the side of the road on a snowy night when we both happened to be going to the same place was like a bolt of lightning out of the sky. I was going to capture the residual charge from that lightning, and I didn't intend to let go.

As I threaded my hand into her hair, it gave easily, sliding like silk between my fingers. With her eyes like fire on mine, I bent my head, brushing my lips across hers, almost as if to test what might happen. This moment was so surreal I wouldn't be shocked if we burst into flames.

Her lips were warm and soft. Electricity hummed around us, my lips almost tingling against hers. A low sound came from her throat, and I distantly heard my own growl in return as I angled my head to the side and fit my mouth over hers.

Delilah sighed, her lips giving way and inviting me in. Sweet hell, she tasted so good. The crisp, cool scent of snow clung to her. Her mouth was warm and sweet, and the moment she let me in, it was just as I had remembered.

Her tongue slipped out to tease against mine. She was no passive kisser, not Delilah. One of her hands slid around my lower back, and she tugged me closer. My arousal nestled perfectly in the cradle of her hips, nudging against her core. She was a tall woman, fitting against me just so, and all soft curves in contrast to my hard planes.

Our kiss started as a slow, sensual tease before it shifted gears, our tongues tangling as it became wet, hot, and messy. I was gripping her hair tightly as one of her hands mapped its way over my chest.

The Delilah I'd kissed before had been young. Our kisses had been those of two untried, wild teenagers who didn't quite know better. And as hot as those kisses had been, they didn't hold a fucking candle to this one.

I knew my way around a woman's mouth now. Even though I'd all but lost my mind and wasn't thinking at all, my years of experience kicked in. By the time I broke free from her mouth, it was out of near desperation for air. I sucked in a breath, opening my eyes just as she did. Our gazes collided, hers hazy and unfocused and likely matching mine.

We stared at each other, the sound of our breath heaving loud in the small space. Blood rushed through my ears with the thundering beat of my pulse pounding through my body.

Delilah's lips were puffy and swollen from our kiss, and her cheeks flushed. I could feel the restless beat of her heart against my chest, and I imagined she could feel mine. We were plastered together with one of her feet hooked around my calves.

Lifting a hand, she traced her fingertip along my cheek-bone, leaving a trail of fire in the wake of her touch. "That was better than I remembered," she breathed.

I felt my lips kicking up into a smile on one side. "I'll say." My words came out gruff.

I had imagined absolutely none of this. I just knew I

wanted a chance to take things to the place we never got to go before. Yet this suddenly felt heavy, weighted with a startling intensity.

Delilah took another breath. When I felt the tight peaks of her nipples press against me, my mouth was on hers again. My body was strung tight with a need so fierce I forgot where we were. I devoured her mouth as her tongue warred with mine. I didn't even feel the elevator shuddering to a stop until the doors opened, and I heard a voice.

"Oops!" a woman's voice exclaimed.

A soft giggle followed from someone else. Delilah and I broke apart, and I caught myself just before I sagged against the wall in the elevator. The shockwave of kissing her slammed into me. Glancing to the side, I found a pair of women who were politely turned away.

"Sorry about that, ladies," I said as I leaned over to snag Delilah's bag.

"We're sorry to interrupt," one of them said. Her eyes flicked from me to Delilah. "Girl, I'd pay money to have a man kiss me the way he was kissing you. You'd better hang on with both hands."

"Yeah, that was a kiss for the ages," the other woman offered.

Delilah bit her lip and chuckled, her cheeks flushing a deeper shade of pink. She stepped out of the elevator in front of me, and I rested my hand on her lower back, needing to touch her. While she had my engine revving so hard I was practically spinning inside, she was also the only thing for me to cling to in the madness of a need that rushed so fiercely I could barely think.

Chapter Five

DELILAH

The subtle, mellow flavor of the wine slid across my tongue. Setting my glass down, I glanced sideways at Alex and tried to catch my breath. I idly wondered if it was possible to end up having a heart attack for being turned on for too long.

My pulse had been idling on high ever since our kiss in the elevator. I'd sort of pulled myself together after the shock of seeing him before that. Then I lost my damn mind.

That kiss had nearly incinerated me, inside and out. I was surprised I didn't collapse after we got caught in the middle of it by our unexpected audience.

My insides were still liquid molten, and my lips tingled. All the while, my pulse galloped along, revving here and there with nothing more than a glance from him. We were having dinner with Holly and Nate, and I was trying to convey a sense of normalcy. I didn't want his sister to think I was crazy.

Alex's question echoed in my mind. *So tell me, Delilah, did you ever wonder what might happen?*

Oh boy, did I ever wonder. I chalked it up to hazy summer memories and convinced myself over the years that

I had put way too much stock in them. Why couldn't I forget Alex Blake and those smokin' hot make-out sessions?

What were the chances that a girl from decidedly humble roots in the nooks and crannies of the Blue Ridge Mountains would luck into a scholarship for two weeks at camp? I could answer that. Not good. Even less likely was the fact that Alex—a teenager from Alaska, a land which seemed like practically another planet to me—would end up there for the same two weeks.

A shiver ran down my spine as the reality of my current situation slammed into me. Of all the people to find me on the highway in the snow, it was Alex Blake.

Even if he hadn't found me and I'd driven myself here, I still would've seen him. Those two short weeks that summer had been some of the best of my life. It wasn't as if we had a grand romance, but he'd been handsome and nice, and I'd crushed on him *hard*. We had a few hot kisses, and they'd been divine.

Hours before camp ended and I boarded the bus to take me to the airport, I'd given him my address, and he'd promised to send me a letter. As bad luck would have it, my dad got us evicted from that apartment while I was away at camp. I didn't have the kind of parents who were organized enough to arrange for mail to be forwarded. If Alex ever sent a letter, I never knew.

"And for you?" a voice asked, intruding into my reverie.

Looking up, I smiled at the waitress. "I'm sorry. Excuse me?"

"I was just asking what you would like for dinner," she said politely.

"Oh, right. I'll take the sesame salmon with asparagus," I replied, glancing down at the menu in front of me.

"Any appetizers?"

"We already ordered the mini crab cakes and halibut strips," Holly offered helpfully from across the table.

"Are they to share? I don't want to assume."

"Of course," Alex replied.

"Okay then, I'm all set," I said as I handed the menu to the waitress.

Once the waitress hurried away, Holly pinned her sharp brown eyes on me. "So, it's convenient that Alex found you on the side of the road. I find it hard to believe you had no idea he would be here this week," she commented.

I *so* did not have the energy for this. But I supposed I had no choice but to deal with it. After taking a fortifying sip of wine, I met her gaze head-on. "Look, think whatever you want. Alex and I did meet once before at camp many years ago. It was a complete surprise to encounter him again, but I don't have any ulterior motives. My friends gave me this ski trip because something came up for them."

Alex slid his arm over my shoulders, pausing to take a swallow from his beer. "Seriously, Holl. Don't make this something it isn't. I admit, it's crazy to run into Delilah, but I sure as hell don't mind," he said easily.

Nate, with his boyish charm, nudged Holly in the arm. "Cut them some slack. It's almost Christmas."

I shrugged, fighting the urge to swat Alex's arm off my shoulder. Not because I actually wanted it gone, but rather because I loved the feel of it. I wanted to burrow into him, and I hated feeling weak and vulnerable. I'd had more than enough of that in my life.

Holly sighed. "I'm sorry. I'm just a little protective. Who's the friend who gave you the trip?"

"It's actually Shay Martin. Her brother, Remy, who's also a friend of mine, lives in—"

Holly cut in with a wide smile. "Oh, my God. Remy? Our Remy?"

"Well, I don't know if he's *your* Remy, but he grew up where I did in Stolen Hearts Valley, North Carolina. His sister, Shay, lives there. When Remy and his wife couldn't use this trip, he told Shay, and she told me, and here I am," I explained.

Holly slapped her palm on her chest and sighed. "Remy is the sweetest guy."

Nate rolled his eyes and chuckled. "I'm not so sure Remy would appreciate being described as the 'sweetest.'"

Holly elbowed Nate in the side. "Whatever. It's just wild that Delilah knows Remy."

"So y'all live in the same town as Remy?" I asked.

"Yup. Willow Brook," Alex said when I looked at him. "That's where we're from. Remy landed there a few years ago. Solid guy. He's one of the hotshot firefighters based out of there."

I nodded, my mind spinning over how small the world could be. "That's Remy. Shay misses him like crazy. I kind of can't believe he and his wife gave up this week here. This place is really nice," I said as I let my eyes roam around the restaurant.

It was an upscale ski lodge. The restaurant had glossy wood floors with a high ceiling and exposed beams criss-crossing above. The ski slopes glittered in the darkness through the windows facing the mountains. "I can't wait to see outside in the daylight," I added.

Holly nodded enthusiastically. "Oh, it's gorgeous here. As far as Remy giving up his week here, don't feel bad for him. I know for a fact he and Rachel have already been down here twice this winter and have another trip planned in February."

"Well, it's sure nice. I guess, in the end, they didn't give me their week, seeing as the room wasn't even available," I said with a little laugh.

"I hope you're giving Delilah the bed," Holly said with a pointed look at Alex.

His fingers were lightly teasing the hair at the nape of my neck, sending little shivers down my spine that were swirling into the ache building between my thighs. My body's reaction to Alex was off the charts, and here, I had his sister's protective gaze trained on us. I sensed her claws would come out if she thought it necessary.

"When did you two meet before?" Nate asked after the waitress arrived with our appetizers.

"Remember that camp I went to for a few summers?" Alex said between bites of the crispy and delicious halibut strips.

"Oh, yeah. You loved that. You got to go fly-fishing and whatnot on the lake in the mountains. I don't even remember where it was," Holly said.

"Colorado," I offered, my mind spinning back to one afternoon. Those two short weeks lived in my memory as a haze of sunshine and warmth. The heat in Colorado was nothing like the heat of North Carolina where the humidity was so heavy it clung to your skin sometimes. I loved the cool waters of that lake in Colorado and Alex's rich brown eyes.

My heart leaped when the cold water splashed on my skin. I was sitting on a dock by myself one afternoon almost halfway through my time there. Plenty of kids attended the camp, but it wasn't too hard to get away. I loved to hide away and read and had found a floating dock tucked off to the side of the main swimming area. The voices of the other kids frolicking in the water carried over to me, but I felt as if I'd found my own special sanctuary.

Alex smiled at me as he rose from the water. "I thought that was you," he said.

His hands curled over the edge of the floating wooden raft as he pulled himself onto it. It rocked slightly with his weight. I closed my book and rolled up from where I'd been lying down.

Alex was handsome, the kind of handsome that was almost too much. His body was lean and muscled. He smiled again as he ran his hand over his wet hair. A few droplets landed on my legs and sent shivers chasing through me.

"Do you like to read?" he asked.

"I do. It's my favorite thing, actually."

Guys usually left me tongue-tied, especially guys as handsome as

Alex, but there was something about him. He was just easy to be with. He was also so removed from my life back home that I didn't have to worry about what he might think about me.

He had no idea that my parents were poor, and my father screamed at us most of the time. Or that the stolen moments alone with him were the only ones I'd ever had with a guy. Most guys back home steered clear of me. Fashionable, I was not. I often wore the same clothes over and over because I didn't have enough to get me through the week.

When my best friend found out I won the scholarship to camp, she had promptly handed over every single pair of cutoffs she had. Between the two of us, I had exactly enough to get me through these two weeks at camp.

It was a lucky accident that cutoffs were in fashion this summer. It was also lucky that it was totally okay to only have two bikini tops and a few tank tops. Most girls wore the same tops over and over at camp.

Alex angled toward me, hooking one foot under his knee. "I bet you're a straight A student."

I totally was, and almost no one ever cared.

I flashed a shy smile and shrugged. "Maybe. So tell me where you're from."

"Alaska."

"Really? Wow. That's crazy."

"It's not as crazy as it sounds. Where are you from?"

"North Carolina."

"Alaska is beautiful, but the mountains here are beautiful too. I bet the mountains in North Carolina are pretty too."

"They are, just a lot smaller."

I didn't realize it, but somehow, we were sitting pretty close together. When he leaned forward, a hum of electricity zinged between us. Alex had already stolen two kisses from me, and just now I saw his gaze lingering on my mouth.

"You make me a little crazy, Delilah," he said, his voice low and husky.

Butterflies spun in my belly, and I felt shivery all over. "Kiss me again," I breathed.

"All you had to do was ask."

He leaned forward, his lips brushing across mine. That electricity centered on our lips now, the force sizzling between us. I heard a sound coming from my throat and then Alex was leaning closer, pulling me into his lap. Although I knew I should think what we were doing was naughty, it didn't feel that way with him.

As I straddled his knees and rocked my hips over the hard ridge of his arousal, we kissed like the crazy young teenagers we were. There wasn't much skill to it. It was wet and messy.

Alex was the one who broke away. "Delilah," he murmured, his hands sliding down my sides to grab my hips and hold them still. "We have to stop."

"But I don't want to."

Chapter Six

DELILAH

That memory flashed through my mind as I glanced up when Alex said something. I had *totally* lost track of the conversation.

My smile seemed to be enough to gloss it over. "So what do you do?" Holly's question punctured the haze left behind by my old summer memories.

Looking toward her, I replied, "I'm a bartender. I made it through college, but not as fast as I wanted, mostly because I've been working the whole time. I'm doing online nursing classes now. Hopefully, I'll get my nursing degree someday."

I waited for a hint of disapproval. I was accustomed to people not thinking much of what I did, but my cynical expectation was proven wrong. Holly's eyes widened. "Oh, that's great. I'm a nurse. That must be hard, trying to do classes online while you're working. I have nothing but respect for anyone who can pull that off. I'm so glad to be done with nursing school. If you need any pointers, ask away."

"When it comes time for my nursing exam, I just might take you up on that," I said.

While I attempted to have some sort of normal social conversation, all the while, Alex's fingers were brushing back and forth just above the collar of my shirt on my neck. That tiny patch of skin was on fire with streaks radiating through my body. I could feel the wet silk between my thighs. If he kept this up, I was going to tackle him in the elevator. We hadn't discussed it, but I'd made a decision after that crazy hot kiss earlier.

I might never see Alex after this, but I was going to see things through in the way I'd never been able to before.

I got through dinner with polite conversation and even sat through a round of introductions to a bunch of people Holly, Nate, and Alex knew from Diamond Creek. They were on a friendly basis with the owners of the lodge, the woman who managed the restaurant, and a few others who stopped by to say hello.

By the time we got to the elevator, I was contemplating whether I could actually orgasm merely from sitting beside Alex for that long. Once the elevator doors closed, I reached for Alex's hand and reeled him closer.

"Okay, here's the deal. You were such a fucking gentleman back when we were at camp that you never let anything go too far. It's been over a decade, and now you have no excuses," I said, lightly tapping my index finger on the center of his chest.

Alex's gaze darkened, and he ran his tongue across his teeth as his lips kicked up into a half smile. "It sounds like we're on the same page. Gotta say, though, I never thought I'd get a lecture for being a gentleman. We were young."

"I guess I can appreciate that. Then, but not now."

At that, I tugged him closer. He didn't hesitate to fit his mouth over mine. We dived right back to where our kiss left off before, and Alex took control almost instantly. The not as experienced young man he'd been before had given way to a demanding, commanding man, and I loved it.

Chapter Seven

ALEX

Delilah was warm and soft, and her mouth held a lingering plum flavor from the wine. Her scent spun around me like a drug. A drug just for me, and I'd been hooked for years even though I hadn't seen her in all that time.

Her tongue slicked against mine, and I tightened my grip in her hair as she arched into me. When she let out a little moan, I growled in return.

Delilah stripped away any artifice, taking everything down to a pure, elemental level.

I needed her closer. *Now.* Stepping back slightly and breaking free from our kiss to gulp in air, I lifted her against me. She didn't hesitate, winding her legs around my hips as she trailed a fingertip along the stubble on my jaw.

"Just one night," she murmured.

"Oh, Delilah, there will be far more than just one night."

We stared at each other. I knew what I felt. Back when I was barely a man, and she was barely a woman, I had no doubt about the way I felt when I was with her. It was just *right*. Years passed, and I figured I'd never see her again. All along, I occasionally wondered if my memory played tricks on me.

Until I saw her again, then there was no wondering anymore. My memory had been spot-on. Maybe only an evening had passed since our worlds collided again, but it felt as if a missing piece in the puzzle of my life had clicked into place.

Holding her and turning to press her back against the wall, I adjusted her in my arms. I lifted a hand to trace my thumb along the elegant slope of her cheekbone and down around her plump lips. "I know it's not just me. So let's not pretend this doesn't feel the way it does," I rasped.

The Delilah I remembered had a guarded, careful sense to her. That quality had hardened a bit, and she had an almost harsh quality to her defenses now. While I didn't know the story of her life, I knew *her*, the person underneath, the woman who called to me all those years ago and who called to me even more powerfully now.

Vulnerability flickered in her gaze right when I felt the elevator come to a smooth stop. Without ever looking away from her, I reached to the side and jammed my thumb on the center button to keep the doors closed. I wasn't letting this moment get cut short because it was too important.

"Alex," she breathed, the husky sound of her voice only serving to spin the lust driving me even tighter. "That's crazy."

I shook my head. "No. It's not. I was half in love with you then, and I never forgot you, Delilah. I know our lives are worlds apart, but I refuse to pretend this is just a quick, hot night. I know you feel it too," I insisted.

I caught her hand where it rested on my chest between us and flattened her palm over my heart, holding it there. My heart thumped hard and true.

"You don't really know me," she said, her voice soft. Her mouth twisted to the side, and sadness shadowed her gaze, dark clouds drifting through.

"Maybe I don't know all the details, just as you don't know the details of my life. I'm not asking you to make promises. I just don't want to go into this under false pretenses."

The air surrounding us shimmered, weighted with years of desire and brushed with hazy memories colliding with the present and creating sparks. Delilah's lips parted with a soft breath before she nodded.

As she had aptly pointed out, there was much I didn't know about her. Yet I knew she was the kind of woman who held her cards so close to her chest, sometimes she didn't even play the hand. I felt a hint of victory at the flash of desire reflected in her eyes. I leaned forward to catch her lips with mine. We seemed incapable of anything other than hot, wild, and wet kisses because what I meant to be a brief touch instantly morphed when her tongue darted out to tease mine.

The elevator dinged, indicating someone was pushing the buttons on the outside. I tore my lips from hers and eased her down slowly. "Let's get to the room," I murmured, reaching for her hand and holding it tight as I tapped the button, and the elevator doors slid open.

We filed out quickly, and a group of skiers spilled in behind us. Our footsteps were muffled along the carpeted hallway as I all but ran to our room. Delilah kept pace with me easily.

The second the door closed behind us, Delilah turned to face me, tugging her hand free and sliding her hands up under my shirt. My breath hissed through my teeth. My girl might be prickly and guarded, but when she decided to throw herself into something, she was *all* in.

The feel of her palms on my skin spurred me on. We wasted no time, our clothes coming off in a tangle as we made our way to the bed between stumbling kisses and even a giggle from Delilah when she lost her balance as she tried to kick one of her boots off. I thanked the stars the lodge had recently added a small store that sold travel items. I tossed a condom on the bed from the small box I'd purchased earlier.

I was down to my briefs when I looked up and saw her sifting her fingers through her messy hair. The sight of her struck me hard, right at my core.

Delilah was breathtaking. With her glossy, almost black hair that she didn't even bother to style, her rich green eyes, and her bold features, high cheekbones, a strong jaw, and dark brows that arched slightly. She exuded strength with only her full lips softening the clean angles of her face. When she was younger, she had a softer look to her, yet she was even more beautiful now. To me.

I'd never seen her bare naked, and she wasn't quite there now, but I'd seen her in a bikini almost every day for those two weeks of camp. Still, my memory had been veiled and gauzy with time washing away its crispness. She'd filled out more, her breasts generous and her hips flaring out. She had a soft curve to her belly, and I wanted to kiss it. Her legs were long and muscular. Her eyes met mine when they traveled back to her face.

She had one hand curled over the edge of her panties, and I shook my head. "Not yet," I said. "Come here."

She didn't hesitate, closing the distance between us and stopping in front of me where I stood at the foot of the bed. My arousal filled my boxer briefs, making them tight. I knew it was obvious, and I didn't give a damn.

"So, tell me—honestly, this time—did you ever wonder?" I asked.

Delilah's eyes searched my face. Her teeth sank into the corner of her bottom lip, denting it and making me want to dive back into the warm sweetness of her mouth.

She nodded slowly. "Of course, I did. Just so you know, if you ever sent me a letter, my parents got evicted from our apartment while I was at camp, so I never got any mail from there."

I filed that tidbit away in the parking lot of my mind to ask her about later. I had only a sketch of her life but sensed it hadn't been easy. "I *did* send you a letter, and I wondered why you never wrote back."

Her shoulders rose with a breath, falling slowly as she let it out. "They lost my luggage on the way back, so I didn't have your address either. I'm sorry," she said quietly.

I recalled asking for her phone number so we could text, but she didn't own a phone. I was starting to grasp just how little she might have had.

"It's okay," I said, stepping closer. "I've decided it was meant to happen this way."

She took another step, closing the last bit of distance between us, her nipples teasing me through the black lace of her bra as they brushed against me when she leaned up and slid her hand around the back of my neck. I needed no convincing. My mouth was on hers in a hot second, devouring her. I wanted to feel *all* of her all at once, but it wasn't quite possible. I made do with sliding my hand down her back to cup her lush bottom, savoring her low moan when I gave it a little squeeze. When I nudged my knee between her thighs, a wash of satisfaction rolled through me when I felt the damp silk against my leg.

Blazing a trail of kisses down her neck and savoring the salty tang of her skin, I murmured against her as I teased my fingers between her thighs. "You're soaked, Delilah. Is that all for me?"

She gasped when I nipped lightly at her skin just below the base of her throat. I teased my fingers over the wet silk, pressing lightly over her clit, swollen enough to be obvious even through her panties.

"What do you think?" she teased in return.

I chuckled, feeling goose bumps rise on her skin under my lips as I made my way down between her breasts. "I vote yes," I said right before I sucked one of her tight nipples into my mouth. She cried out, spearing her fingers in my hair as I swirled my tongue around it before turning my attention to her other breast.

Seeing as I hadn't expected to see Delilah ever again, all my fantasies about her were blurry. Having her here in my arms—a living, breathing flame with her skin dewy and every sound she made driving me wild—I lost all ability to orchestrate this.

I needed her bare naked and tangled up with me. Only then might I be able to shackle the lust driving me with a force that couldn't be denied.

Lifting my head, I flicked the clasp between her breasts, almost groaning aloud when her breasts tumbled free, her nipples rosy and damp from my attentions. She gave her shoulders a little shimmy, and the bra fell to the floor beside us.

Lifting her, I set her hips on the bed, then leaned my hands on either side, my face no more than an inch away from hers. "Now's your chance," I said, my voice husky with need.

"My chance for what?"

I didn't miss the subtle shift of her thighs and imagined her folds sliding back and forth because she was so fucking wet.

"To tell me you don't want this."

Her thighs shifted again, her eyes holding mine as she shook her head.

"Is that a 'no, you don't want this,' or 'no, you don't want to take that chance'?"

She lifted a hand, tracing her fingertip over my lips. "Back to your earlier question, I'm soaked for *you*."

Fuck me. I didn't think it was possible to have the upper hand with Delilah, not when I was all but a slave to my need for her, but I didn't care.

I gave her a fierce kiss before pressing her thighs apart and coming down on my knees in front of her. The silk of her panties was drenched when I trailed my fingers over it.

Watching her face, I savored the sight of her biting her lip when a little whimper escaped as I hooked my finger in the edge of the silk and pushed it out of the way. Her pussy was pink, wet, and glistening.

I didn't wait, leaning forward and licking her folds as she cried out sharply, one hand fisting the comforter and the other clinging to my hair. I sank one finger and then another into her slick channel as I tasted her very essence. She was so responsive, gasping loudly and murmuring my name raggedly as her channel clenched around my fingers.

In a matter of seconds, I could feel her racing to the edge as the tremors increased in intensity. I swirled my tongue around her clit and sucked it lightly. Her entire body went taut. "Alex!" she cried, yanking my hair hard enough it stung a little. I couldn't have cared less. I welcomed the pain.

Lifting my head, I let myself soak in the sight of her. Her skin was dewy, and her breasts rose and fell with every ragged breath. Her eyes finally opened, her gaze dark and hazy.

"I need you inside me," she said flatly.

Now, *that* was a program I could get with. Rising, I shoved my briefs down and reached for the condom I'd tossed on the bed while she shimmied out of her panties and kicked them free from her ankles. I rolled the condom on before lowering a knee to the bed.

She shifted back as I rose over her. "Hold on," I murmured, trying to ease my weight down carefully.

"Oh no, you don't," she gasped roughly.

I couldn't hold back the huff of laughter that escaped. "Don't worry, we're not stopping. I just want the best way to see you come on my cock."

Delilah bit her lip when I rolled us over, resting my back up against the pillows. She got right with me, straddling my thighs, her breasts brushing against my chest as she lifted her hips slightly.

"We can go slow next time," she murmured as she reached between us, positioning my cock at her entrance.

When I felt the kiss of slick arousal from her pussy, my head thumped against the headboard, and I grabbed her hips tightly. She sheathed me slowly in her core, her snug, clenching heat nearly pushing me over the edge instantly. When she sank down fully and I was buried to the hilt inside her, she lifted her eyes.

It felt as if a bolt of electricity passed between us. Being inside Delilah was like coming home. Nothing had ever felt so right in my life.

Her eyes widened before she settled her hips again, rocking slightly. "Alex," she breathed.

"I know."

Chapter Eight

DELILAH

As I stared into Alex's dark eyes, my heart was thudding so hard and fast inside my chest that every beat echoed throughout my entire body. The slick fusion of our joining felt almost surreal, primal, and elemental.

It had been a while—quite a while—since I'd had sex. Alex was thick and long, stretching me enough that it burned slightly even though I was no virgin.

Tears stung the back of my eyes as emotion crashed over me. There was desire, and then there was this—this fierce, epochal intensity I felt with Alex.

Alex held still, the feel of his fingers pressing into my skin about the only anchor in the storm of sensation and emotion swirling within me. He eased his grip on one hip, his hand sliding up my side and his thumb briefly teasing my nipple, tight and achy. Then he brushed my hair away from my face.

"Delilah," he murmured gruffly.

Although I felt as if I were spun loose inside, when I looked into his eyes, there was a sense of settling, an ease and a rightness to this moment. Leaning forward slightly, I pressed my lips to his, just a brush of a kiss. Electricity sizzled between our lips, and his hand laced into my hair. His tongue teased mine, slow and sensual, as he rocked his hips, seating himself more deeply.

I gasped when my clit pressed against his pelvis with just enough friction to send a sharp burst of pleasure spinning through me. He leaned his head back against the headboard when I broke away with another gasp.

His gaze was heavy-lidded, containing an intensity that set my heart pounding even harder. His hand slipped free from my hair to grab my hips again as I surrendered to the urge to move.

Rising up, I then sank down over his length again, sheathing him inside my core and crying out as he rose to meet me. I was so close. Each time I rocked into him, the pleasure rippled through me like a wave rolling into itself. I felt myself tightening and heard him murmuring my name.

"Come on, baby, let go. I need to feel you fly apart."

He reached between us, teasing his fingers over where we were joined. The wave crashed, wracking my body with pleasure as I shuddered around him. I felt him tighten, his hand gripping my hip as he cried out my name in a rough shout. I felt the heat of his cock pulsing inside me as I collapsed against him, his arms coming around me and holding me close.

As I gradually caught my breath, I felt the beat of his heart against mine. I was spent and utterly sated. Pleasure pinged through me in tiny aftershocks. I didn't want to move. Ever.

After we untangled ourselves, Alex sweet-talked me into taking a shower with him. Not that it took much effort, mind you.

I fell asleep with one of my legs tucked over his, and his arm wrapped around my shoulders, holding me tight against him.

Chapter Nine

ALEX

The lights outside the windows illuminated the falling snow at the ski lodge. Delilah laughed at something before pausing to take a sip of her wine.

"I'm going to run to the restroom," Delilah said when she set her glass down. "Be right back."

The moment Delilah was out of earshot, my sister caught my eyes. "Delilah is awesome, and you are whipped," Holly said with a wide grin, her brown eyes sparkling.

"Oh, he's not just whipped," Nate added. "You, my man, are seriously falling for her."

I shrugged, not feeling any need to argue the point. "I am. I just have to convince Delilah it's not crazy." Holly's eyes were bright. "Are you gonna cry on me?"

Nate grinned, slipping his arm around her shoulders and pressing a kiss to her cheek. "She gets all emotional when it comes to love. You know that."

"Do you think she would move here?" Holly asked.

"Maybe," I replied, my mind spinning back over the past week. This stolen time over the holidays had blown my mind and heart wide open. What was supposed to be a ski trip with friends and family to enjoy Christmas together had turned into so much more. My nights were filled with Delilah, and I knew I was falling in love with her. I didn't care if it seemed too soon and too crazy.

Our waiter paused to check on us, and I looked up to see Delilah approaching. Her dark hair gleamed under the holiday lights strewn about the restaurant. When her eyes met mine across the room, my heart kicked hard against my ribs.

Hours later, Delilah stood in front of the windows in our room, the snow falling lightly outside. I lifted the sprig of mistletoe that Marley had allowed me to steal from the lodge restaurant. I'd assured her it was for a good cause.

Stopping beside Delilah, I slipped one hand around her waist from behind, dropping my head into the sweet curve of her neck where I pressed a few kisses.

"Hey," I murmured.

"Hey, you," she replied, the soft twang in her voice familiar now. I'd fallen so hard for her I didn't quite know what to do about it.

When she angled her head back to look at me, I held up the mistletoe. "I think this means you need to kiss me."

Her lips curled in a smile as her shoulders shook with laughter. "Since when did you need mistletoe to get me to kiss you?"

"I was going for the holiday spirit." I dropped another kiss on her neck before lifting my head to catch her lips with mine, savoring the curve of her smile right before I swept my tongue in her mouth. "Merry Christmas," I murmured with a smile when I drew away.

She angled her head to the side, her smile stretching wide. "Merry Christmas."

Chapter Ten

ALEX

January

"Delilah, it doesn't have to be that way," I pressed.

Delilah's dark lashes swept up, her clear green gaze searching my face. My heart felt squeezed tight. Although we'd had two incredible weeks together, my girl wasn't falling for the idea we could make this something more than a vacation fling.

Her lips twisted to the side, and she lifted her hand, lightly tracing her thumb along my jawline. "Alex, you live here. In Alaska. I live in North Carolina. Those places are far apart. The past two weeks have been incredible, and I'll never forget them, but let's not be ridiculous."

I let her bag slide free from my hand. The soft thump of it hitting the tiled floor at the airport felt like an echo to my heartbeat. Stepping closer, I trailed my fingers through the ends of her dark silky hair and slid my other arm around her waist as I brought her body flush with mine.

"It's not ridiculous," I insisted.

A look I had come to know well passed through her eyes, like shadows blotting out the sun. "I suck at goodbyes," she muttered. Dropping her gaze from mine, she pressed her forehead against my chest, just above my heart. I felt her hand slide up and down my back, almost as if she was trying to comfort me.

When she lifted her face again, her eyes were shuttered, her chin set in a stubborn line. "I'll miss you," she said simply before she leaned up and pressed her lips to mine quickly.

"I'll miss you too." I tried to hold her, but Delilah was clearly determined not to drag this moment out.

She stepped back abruptly and grabbed her bag. "I'll call you when I land."

"Delilah—" I began.

She walked away backward, pressing her fingertips against her lips and blowing me a kiss. "I'll miss you, Alex," she called.

I began to move in her direction, but unfortunately, I had already walked as far as I could with her. We were just outside the security section at the airport. A somber security agent held up his palm. "Sorry, sir, you'll need to wait back here unless you're a traveling passenger."

Feeling defeated, I watched as Delilah walked away. The airport in Anchorage wasn't crowded this morning. It was only a few minutes before her dark head disappeared after she went through security. She never once looked back.

Turning away, I walked through the airport, a sense of melancholy settling over me. When I stepped outside, it was still dark, and the air was bitingly cold. January in Anchorage was never warm. I'd guess it was close to zero with the wind-chill this morning.

It would be several hours before the sun came up. For now, the stars glittered above as I climbed into my truck and began the drive back to Willow Brook.

I didn't know how, but I was going to convince Delilah it was worth seeing where this thing between us went.

———

"I'm all about love, Alex, but you can't expect Delilah to think it's worth trying a long-distance relationship without telling her how you feel," Holly said.

"I did tell her how I feel," I protested.

"How you feel about who?" Janet asked as she stopped beside our table and set down my bagel with cream cheese and Holly's croissant.

"Alex is in love, but he won't say the L word," Holly said tartly before taking a bite of her croissant and leaving me to face Janet's curious gaze.

We were having breakfast at Firehouse Café. Janet was the owner, and I'd known her my entire life. Her silver braid was spun into a circle on top of her head, and her round cheeks plumped with her smile when she looked at me.

"You're in love? I need the scoop. And how come I haven't heard about this sooner?" Janet prompted.

I didn't even try to hide my sigh. "When we went to the ski lodge in Diamond Creek over the holidays, I ran into a girl I knew back in high school."

"Oh, she's from Willow Brook?" Janet returned.

I refused to look at my sister because I knew she was enjoying putting me on the spot like this. "No, Delilah's not from Willow Brook. I met her one summer when I went to camp in Colorado."

"And you both ended up at Last Frontier Lodge together over Christmas? Oh, it feels like fate." Janet put her hand on her chest over her heart as she looked at me, practically getting misty-eyed.

I took a gulp of my coffee before replying, "She doesn't feel that way. She went back to North Carolina and thinks it's ridiculous that I want to try to have a long-distance relationship."

Holly had finished chewing and helpfully offered her feedback. "But Alex didn't tell Delilah he's in love with her," she said pointedly. "I told him he can't expect her to want to try this when he's not putting his feelings on the line."

"Thanks for your input," I muttered.

Janet looked between us with an affectionate grin. "Maybe he wasn't ready. All you can do is try," she said just as someone called her name from the kitchen. With a pat on my shoulder, she hurried away.

Holly's assessing brown eyes held mine. "She's right. All you can do is try."

"Why are you jumping so fast to the word love?" I asked, honestly curious. I didn't want to contemplate how my neck felt a little itchy just thinking about the word.

"Because I've never seen you like this with a woman. Ever. Maybe it is early, and I get it. But you can't expect someone to want to put effort into a relationship when you two are that far apart if you don't let her know you're *seriously* serious."

I took a bite of my bagel, chewing as I contemplated her words. After I finished, I nodded. "I get your point. I'm not sure how to go about it, but I'm gonna call Delilah tonight."

Holly finished off her croissant and set her empty coffee mug on the plate. "Good. Meanwhile, I have to go to work."

Holly stood from the table, putting a jacket on over her outfit of scrubs. She was a nurse at the ER department in Willow Brook. With a quick smile and a wave, she hurried off. I finished my bagel alone, wishing Delilah was here with me.

"Alex!" a voice called. It was hours later, and I was busy at work.

I didn't recognize the voice because I had my head buried in the engine compartment of a small plane. I tightened the bolt on the part I'd just replaced. Stepping back, I straightened and snagged the rag on the stool beside me to wipe my hands.

Looking up, I saw Nate approaching. "There you are," he said as he crossed from the door of the plane hangar over to where I was working.

"Yes, here I am," I teased as I tossed the rag to the floor and picked up my water bottle to take a swallow. "What's up?"

"Wondering if you have some extra time today to look at one of my planes. Problem with a cooling fan."

"Of course. I always have time for you."

Nate grinned. "I never like to assume."

"Dude, we've been best friends since we were kids, and now you're married to my sister. Holly would kick my ass if I didn't make time for you."

Nate shrugged. "Maybe so. I'll still pay you."

I chuckled. "I know. I'm not that much of a sucker." Glancing at my watch, I added, "I actually have time now. Today is a light day for me. Let me wash my hands, and we can walk on over to your hangar now."

"Sounds good." Nate walked with me as I crossed over to an industrial sink in the corner. I quickly soaped my hands with the citrus cleaner that would break up the grime from working on engines all morning. As an airplane mechanic in Alaska, I was lucky enough to be able to run my own business and basically take the work I wanted. Alaska had a network of small airports—using the term "airport" loosely —due to how many areas of the state were off the road system.

I had contracts with the main airline carriers in Anchorage and Fairbanks, but my bread and butter came from working on small planes scattered across Southcentral Alaska. Nate was a pilot, as was I, but I was purely recreational. He ran a business doing flight work for the hotshot firefighters based out of Willow Brook. He was one of the many pilots who fought fires from the air, dropping flame retardant and water in hot spots when fires got started during the long, dry summers in Alaska.

Nate had several planes he kept stored at the Willow Brook airport. He led me over to the main hangar that housed two of his planes.

"What do you think the problem is?" I asked as he opened the engine compartment.

"Not sure. The fan just doesn't sound right. I'm keeping it out of commission this week until you have a chance to look at it."

"Let me see." A moment later, I could see the loose bolt holding the fan in place. A closer look revealed it was rusting. "You were right about the sound. I'm guessing that's throwing off the rotation just a tad." I commented. "I'll replace the fan later. It's just the bolt, but it's smarter to replace the whole thing. I happen to have one in stock."

Nate's stomach growled audibly as I straightened. "Are you hungry?" I teased.

"Didn't my stomach just answer your question?" He rolled his eyes.

I chuckled. I supposed so. "Why don't we go grab lunch? I'll take care of this fan later this afternoon."

In short order, for the second time this week, I settled into a chair at a small round table in Firehouse Café. The restaurant choices in Willow Brook weren't particularly extensive, and Firehouse Café was my favorite. It was housed in the town's original firehouse and had been renovated into a cute little café with stained concrete floors, artwork on the walls, and Janet's friendly presence.

She approached our table with a wide smile for both of us. "Hey, boys, wanna hear the specials?"

"Always," Nate replied.

Janet rattled off the specials. As soon as she was done, I said, "I'll take the balsamic maple salmon burger with regular fries."

"I'll take the same," Nate added.

"Any coffee?" Janet returned as she jotted down our orders on her small notepad.

"Sure thing. Just the house coffee will do."

After Nate nodded in agreement, Janet hurried off. The café was busy this afternoon, but that was the case every day it was open.

"Holly tells me you miss Delilah," Nate began, jumping straight to the one thing I'd barely been able to stop thinking about.

"You know, the biggest downside to you two being together is now you tell each other everything. Used to be you barely talked to each other," I muttered.

Nate cast me a cheeky grin. "So what? That's not my point. My point is what the hell are you gonna do about Delilah?"

If I was going to talk to anyone about this, it was Nate. "When she left, I tried to talk her into—"

Nate cut right in. "Yeah, some kind a long-distance thing. Dude, you're in Alaska, and she's in North Carolina. The way I see it, if you want this thing to be real in the long run, then somehow she comes here, or you go there."

I didn't know how to label the emotion that jolted me. It was a mixture of anticipation and anxiety, and maybe tinged with a hint of fear. I wasn't used to putting things on the line. Frankly, I never even considered it when it came to a relationship.

Yet Delilah had haunted my memories ever since that summer. It's just until our worlds collided again, I'd written it off as a fluke. Was I actually going to let her go?

Nate's gaze went somber as he stared across the table at me.

"You're not joking, are you?" I prompted.

"No. You're my best friend. I wouldn't joke about something like this. I don't want you to move to North Carolina, but it's obvious Delilah means a lot to you. I think it'd be stupid to let her slip away."

"Since when did you become an expert on romance?" I tried to deflect.

Nate cocked his head to the side, a knowing glint in his gaze. "I'm not claiming to be an expert, although I'm more of an expert than you. You've never been serious about anyone. I do know you well, and I can tell this has gotten to you. Do something about it."

"I want to," I said, running a hand through my hair as I leaned back in my chair.

At that moment, Janet arrived with our coffees, setting them down quickly, along with two glasses of water. "Your food will be ready in a few," she said before she hurried away.

Fortunately for me, I was only grilled by Nate this afternoon. Janet was far too busy to join in like she had when I was here at breakfast.

"It's just I can't imagine moving to North Carolina. I love my life here," I commented after a few sips of coffee.

Nate took a swallow of his coffee, his thumb tracing the handle of the mug as he looked over at me when he set it down. "Nothing's a given. But if you want Delilah to consider you as something other than a fling over the holidays, you've got to be willing to put something on the line. I'll be honest, I think it's worth trying, but there's no way I could do a long-term situation where Holly was thousands of miles away, and I was here. I'd fucking move if that's what it took to be with her. All you can do is be willing to try to consider the possibilities."

I stared over at my oldest friend and slowly nodded. "I'll think about it."

Chapter Eleven

DELILAH

February

I tapped the button to turn off my car. The engine stopped rumbling, and quiet settled around me. The trees had a light dusting of snow; their branches stripped bare of leaves and stark against the gray sky. In front of me sat my parents' house.

They'd actually been living in this house for five years now, the longest length of time they'd lived anywhere. Shockingly, they owned it and the small piece of property on which it sat. I drew a kernel of comfort from that.

That comfort came with a prick of grief. They had this house and piece of property because my grandmother had left it to my mother in her will when she passed away. I missed my gram deeply. She'd been the most stable force in my entire childhood. The second I thought about her, Alex came to mind.

It almost annoyed me that I remembered him when I thought of her now. Gram was the reason I went to that camp in Colorado in high school. She'd sat with me and helped me finish the application. My guidance counselor had wisely sent the paperwork to her instead of my parents. Because my parents hadn't been stable enough to stay in one place when I was growing up. Now that they didn't have to pay rent, it didn't matter.

Thinking of Alex sent a shaft of longing through me, so piercing I felt a physical ache around my heart. I took several deep breaths and willed the pain away.

My car door creaked a little as I pushed it open. The snow-covered dead leaves crunched under my boots as I approached the front porch. I knocked lightly before turning the knob and calling, "Mom? Dad? It's me."

"Hey, darlin'," my mom called from the kitchen.

I closed the door behind me, letting my eyes scan the familiar living room. All the furnishings were the same as when my grandmother was alive. There was an overstuffed couch and two chairs flanking it. She'd loved that sort of country living feel. There were cute curtains with cherries on them. Everything was a little dusty.

My mother's face appeared in the archway between the living room and kitchen. "Coffee?"

"I'd love some." I tapped the snow off my boots and toed them off by the door as I unzipped my jacket.

My mother was filling two mugs with coffee at the counter when I entered the kitchen. "Sit," she said, gesturing toward the round table by the windows.

The view here was lovely. This little piece of property sat on one side of Stolen Hearts Valley. The Blue Ridge Mountains stretched in the distance, and the valley spilled out beyond the edge of the yard. The famed blue haze was shades of gray and silver today. Looking at the mountains also brought Alex to mind.

The stark, magnificent mountains in Alaska were just as beautiful as the Blue Ridge Mountains, yet they felt so different. Here, it felt as if you were cradled in the embrace of the rolling hills. In Alaska, the mountains stood tall and dark against the sky. As an almost otherworldly and massive presence, they were breathtaking in their ability to make you feel so utterly small and human.

I kicked thoughts of Alex to the curb in my mind. He wasn't making it easy to forget him, though. He texted me every single day and also called every single night. I loved it and hated how much I loved it.

My mother sat down across from me, brushing her dark hair streaked with silver away from her eyes. We shared the same coloring. Her clear green eyes were as bright as ever. "How are things?" she asked as she passed over my mug of plain black coffee.

"Fine. Busy." I took a sip, appreciating the rich flavor. "Good coffee," I added as I lowered my mug to the table.

"You've been melancholy ever since you got back from Alaska," she commented.

"I have?" I hedged.

My mother was too perceptive for my sanity. After a childhood of her being somewhat flighty and far too easy to cave to my father's careless whims, my mother had settled down, and we were slowly trying to build something of a relationship.

She cocked her head to the side, tapping her index finger on the table lightly. "Yes, you have. What happened?"

"Really, Mom? Nothing. I had a good trip, and now it's back to the grind. It was nice to have a break from work and school for two weeks. That's all." I was feeling defensive, and I knew it, but I didn't feel like dwelling on what I couldn't have. "Is Dad up?" I asked, knowing my mother wouldn't appreciate the change of subject.

My mother shook her head. "No. And I'm sure you already thought so."

I felt a pinch of guilt in my chest, a little burn right above my heart. Because I *did* know that. "Mom, why do you stay?" I whispered.

She took a swallow of her coffee and let out an almost imperceptible sigh when she set her mug back on the table. "I know your father hasn't made your life easy. I regret many of the things that happened when you were a little girl." She held my gaze with a level look across the table. "He's sick now. Although maybe he doesn't deserve it, I find I can't simply abandon him now."

My stomach felt hollow. "What do you mean, he's sick?"

"We found out before your trip, but I didn't want to tell you because I didn't want you not to go. I haven't seen you for more than a few minutes since you got back. He has cancer, colon cancer. It's pretty far along. Lord knows, your father was never one to go to the doctor. I wish I'd been able to give you more stability, but I was young and not so strong. I'm sorry."

"Mom, you don't need—" I began.

She shook her head sharply, and I went silent.

"I *do* need to apologize. You're an amazing woman, and I am so proud of you. You're taking care of yourself, you're a hard worker, you're putting yourself through nursing school on your own, but more than that, you're a kind and generous person. Don't think for a second I'm not incredibly proud of you. I also know you beat the odds. If it weren't for my mother, your grandmother, things might not have turned out the way they did for you. Here we are now, and I do believe in doing the right thing. I pray every night about what to do. I find that I won't be able to live with myself if I don't ease the last few months your father has."

This was probably the single most honest conversation I'd ever had with my mother about what our life had been when I was growing up. I'd always loved my mother. I also loved my father, despite his tendency toward chronic alcoholism and careless words. Fortunately, he was mostly a harmless drunk.

The hollow feeling in my stomach intensified, and my

pulse was running along at a shallow, unsteady beat. "Months?"

My mother nodded. "Yes. They gave him four to six months. It's far enough along that they don't recommend chemo. He doesn't want chemo anyway. These days, he sleeps in because he's tired and he feels sick, not because he's hungover."

My mother delivered that information, her eyes resigned and steely. I curled my hands around my coffee mug as if the warmth of it could anchor me somehow. I'd resented my father for years, and suddenly, my resentment went up in smoke.

"You're doing the right thing," I said, and I meant it.

I knew she was. My mother was such a loyal person, and she stood by her commitments. There were many times I wished she wasn't, but her loyalty was an integral part of her personality.

"I know. I just hope you understand."

"Of course I do."

Reaching for her hand, I gave it a quick squeeze. Her lips curled in a weary smile. "He's usually up for a few hours in the evenings. If you'd like to come by, that would be a good time to see him."

"I have to work tonight, but I have Sunday night off."

My mother nodded and took another swallow of her coffee, the sound loud in the quiet kitchen. I could hear the ticking of the clock above the stove and a crow calling outside in the trees, its call piercing in the cold winter day.

"Now let's talk about something else," my mother began. "If there's one thing I've learned since I found out about your father's diagnosis, it's that it doesn't help at all to dwell on it."

"I met someone," I said impulsively. I suppose my mother's blunt honesty had inspired me although I surprised myself by offering that up.

A small smile teased at the corners of my mother's lips. "Really?"

"His name is Alex, and he lives in Alaska. It's kind of crazy, but you remember that summer I went to camp in Colorado?"

"Of course I do. You loved it. You were so upset we didn't have a forwarding address for the mail. What does this have to do with Alex in Alaska?"

"If you can believe it, I met him at that camp. I figured I'd never see him again. I had a fit about not having a forwarding address because I gave him our address for a letter. If you're wondering, he says he wrote one. Anyway, I got stuck in the snow, and he happened to be the person who stopped to help me."

My mother's brows hitched up. "And? Tell me more."

So I told her about everything—except for the hot sex. I ended with, "And that's that. I'm here, and he's there, and that's too far for any kind of reasonable long-distance relationship."

My mother narrowed her eyes, and she leveled me with a look. "Don't be ridiculous. Why don't you go to Alaska? There's nothing holding you here."

"Mom, you just told me Dad is dying. I'm not gonna just leave. Plus, you're here."

"I am. But we'll stay in touch. Maybe wait until your dad passes, but don't just write this guy off. You told me he wants to give things a shot. Don't be afraid to take a chance."

Chapter Twelve

DELILAH

Don't be afraid to take a chance.

My mother's words had been playing on a loop in my brain all evening. Fortunately, I could literally run this bar with one hand tied behind my back.

I mixed a margarita and pulled a draft beer from the tap as I replayed my conversation with my mother in my brain. "Here you go," I said as I slid the beer in one direction and the margarita in another. I counted out change quickly and kept moving.

Suddenly, the hair on the back of my neck stood, and a jolt of awareness sizzled down my spine. *There's no way Alex is here.*

"Delilah."

I *knew* that voice. A vivid memory of Alex's eyes boring into mine just before my body tightened and he cried my name in a gruff shout flashed in my thoughts.

Don't turn around. You're imagining things.

My body didn't listen, as usual. Turning, I couldn't keep my mouth from falling open when I saw him standing at the corner of the bar. His hair was mussed as if he'd run a hand through it too many times. The second his brown eyes locked with mine, my heart flipped over in my chest and butterflies spun wildly in my belly.

"Damn. Never thought I'd see Delilah shocked," Griffin said from beside my shoulder.

I glanced back at my fellow bartender for the evening, and all I could do was shake my head. My eyes reflexively swung back toward Alex, almost expecting him to go up in smoke.

Gulp. He was still there. In the flesh. He leaned his elbow on the bar, a slow grin unfurling on his face and sending sparks flying through my body. I felt as if I'd been plugged into a socket as a jumble of emotions spun through me.

The most unfamiliar emotion of all—joy. I didn't even know what to do with how happy I was to see him.

Griffin clapped me on the shoulder. "I think you need to take a break."

When I looked back toward him, I saw him looking at Alex, and it was as if they communicated in silence. "Come on back," Griffin said, striding past me where my feet were still frozen in place on the rubber mats laid over the wood floor behind the bar.

Griffin casually lifted a section of the counter, gesturing for Alex to come behind the bar. "Delilah's on break. Actually, her shift is done for the night."

I didn't know what Griffin saw on my face, but I didn't have time to give him hell for anything, much less the mental organization to be on my toes enough to pull it off. I moved in a daze.

In another moment, the door to the back hallway clicked shut behind me, and I looked up into Alex's face. My pulse was skittering, and my body felt as if I were about to levitate off the floor from the force of my physical reaction at his mere presence.

"What—" My question ended in a mumble when Alex stepped to me and pulled me into a full body embrace.

I burrowed my face against his chest and wrapped my arms tightly around his waist, simply breathing him in. Every molecule in my body spun in excitement and then settled into the feel of him. Alex was a touchstone to hold me steady in the maelstrom of the emotional storm inside.

Taking several shaky breaths, I savored the scent of him, crisp and woodsy. Somehow, he carried the scent of snow. "You smell like snow," I said into his chest.

His laughter rumbled through me. "That's because it's snowing outside, sweetheart. I didn't bring the snow with me from Alaska."

I finally lifted my head and leaned back. "What are you doing here?" I finished the question I had started several moments ago.

"I missed you. So I bought a plane ticket, and I came to see you."

Gah. Just hearing his voice sent a hot shiver through me, followed by a rush of emotion so intense, my eyes felt hot from the sting of tears. I wasn't a crier and wasn't about to turn into one, so I took a breath and blinked hard.

"You could've told me you were coming."

Alex shrugged. "Sure, I could've. And you probably would've told me not to bother. I know you, girl."

I suddenly felt bashful, an emotion I didn't experience often. But hardly anyone read me the way Alex did.

Chapter Thirteen

ALEX

My heart was kicking along rapidly as I looked down into Delilah's clear green eyes. She bit her lip, her white teeth denting the plump surface. It felt so good to have her in my arms again.

Every cell in my body felt as if it was on fire while my cock swelled and pressed against my zipper. I couldn't even be romantic around Delilah. Pure lust took over the second I was close to her.

Her eyes searched my face, and her lips slowly curled into a smile. "I'm not easy to surprise," she murmured as her cheeks flushed pink.

"I'd bet not. You're too cynical to believe in surprises."

Her lashes swept down again, and I slid my hand up her back to trail my fingers through her silky, dark hair. "I missed you," I repeated. "In case you didn't notice."

She lifted her head again. "You mean to tell me you don't text all the girls every day?" she teased, her tone light.

I knew Delilah's doubts weren't specific to me, but it still stung. Just a little.

"Definitely not. There's only one girl I met at camp who I never forgot."

The door to the back hallway opened, and Delilah jumped back. The guy who'd told her she was done for the night came through.

"Sorry," he said quickly as he glanced between us. "Need a case of the brewery stout."

Delilah hurried down the hallway, calling over her shoulder, "Alex, this is Griffin. Griffin, Alex."

Griffin flashed me a grin. "Nice to meet you. I can get that, you know," he called to Delilah's back as he followed her down the hall.

She slipped through a door in the hall and returned in another second with a case of beer. "I'm working too. I'm not gonna leave you on your own tonight. It's busy out there."

Griffin glanced at me and then back to Delilah. "Like I said, you're done for the night. I can handle it."

I stayed quiet. I *had* shown up unannounced. I could handle waiting a few hours if Delilah preferred to work. Don't get me wrong, though. I wanted her *all* to myself as soon as possible.

Delilah chewed on her bottom lip as she looked from me to Griffin. He took the case of beer from her, commenting, "Drag her out of here if necessary."

"I'm going, I'm going," she insisted. "Are you sure you don't mind?"

Griffin was already making his way back to the door at the end of the hall. "Hell no, I don't mind. I'll get all the tips."

Delilah rolled her eyes. "Thank you. I owe you one."

As Griffin shouldered through the door, the hum of the collective voices in the bar filled the hallway. The door swung shut, and the sounds were muted again.

Delilah looked over at me before spinning away. "Let me get my coat and purse."

I leaned against the wall and waited. A moment later, she reappeared, sliding her arms into a fluffy down jacket and looping her purse over her shoulder. "Did you drive here?" She stopped in front of me and looked up.

Her question barely registered because I *needed* to kiss her. It couldn't wait another second. Pushing away from the wall, I pulled her back into my arms, lifting a hand to trace my thumb along her jaw. "Missed you," I murmured right before dipping my head and brushing my lips across hers.

It felt as if lightning struck between us, the sensation sending licks of fire everywhere. Delilah let out a soft sigh and arched into me. In a hot second, I angled my head to the side and fit my mouth over hers. Her tongue darted out to tangle with mine as I dove into the warm sweetness of her mouth.

Kissing Delilah was everything. Fierce need slid through my veins as she arched into me. We were both fully clothed with winter jackets on, but by the time I drew away, the searing intensity of that kiss had me feeling stripped bare.

Delilah's eyes had gone dark, and her breath was coming in short pants. All the while, my heartbeat galloped along madly, and I could barely catch my breath.

"We should go," she whispered.

"Lead the way."

———

After a small standoff in the parking lot behind the bar where Delilah worked, I gave in to her insistence that I follow her home in my rental car. I selfishly wanted her right beside me immediately. But Delilah was stubborn, and I didn't think it was worth pushing the issue.

I followed her small car down the road in the darkness. Snow was falling lightly, illuminated like glitter in the headlights. The mountain roads here were winding. I didn't like thinking of her driving them alone when it was snowy and dark like this all winter.

When we arrived at a small apartment complex, I slung my backpack over my shoulder and followed her up the stairs. She flicked on the lights when we stepped inside and turned to look at me. Her gaze was guarded, and she seemed worried. Her hands twirled in the air when she gestured vaguely around the room.

"It's not much. I don't, well, I don't have a lot of money. I try to keep my rent low because I'm doing those online classes," she explained.

Delilah turned away quickly, shrugging out of her jacket and toeing off her boots. "You can hang your coat up." She gestured to a row of hooks on the wall by the door.

I followed her lead, hanging up my jacket and taking off my shoes. Her apartment was small, clean, and tidy. It was one large room with the kitchen and living room together with two doors in the back. I presumed one led to a bathroom and the other to a bedroom.

A window looked out over the street in the darkness. Delilah crossed the room and pulled some gauzy white curtains closed over the window.

"Are you hungry?" she asked as she walked over to the small kitchen where there was a round table. The living room was furnished with a big cream-colored sectional with plenty of cushions and a coffee table.

"Actually, I am," I said. "You don't have to make me anything, though."

"Let's order pizza. There's a place just down the street, and they'll deliver."

I had a late dinner with Delilah. We ordered pizza, and I learned pepperoni was her favorite. Of course it was. Because it was my favorite too.

I learned Lost Deer Brewery had a delicious porter, and I learned I loved sitting on the couch with Delilah's feet over my thighs and the pizza box resting on her legs. We ate pizza and watched a house buying show.

Delilah asked me about my work and Willow Brook. It didn't skip my notice that whenever I asked her questions about her personal life here, she gave me nothing more than the vaguest of answers. She seemed to have mastered the skill of offering just enough information so it didn't seem as if she was avoiding, while never giving much of anything specific.

After we finished about half the pizza, I lifted the box from her thighs and set it on the coffee table. "Come here," I murmured.

"I'm right here." She wiggled her feet encased in bright blue socks as if to emphasize her point.

"Not close enough." I snaked an arm around her waist and tugged her closer.

She giggled. A giggle from Delilah made my heart squeeze, just because she was usually so guarded. She landed with her knees on either side of my thighs. Perfect.

I brushed her hair away from her face. "So I thought we should set some ground rules."

"Ground rules?" One of her dark brows rose in a slash.

"Yeah. I'm your unexpected guest, but I do have some manners. Don't change your work schedule for me. I actually arranged some work at the airport in Asheville. I'll be here for two weeks. I'm hoping you'll let me spend every night with you."

Delilah's mouth fell open in a pretty little O. "You're here for two weeks? You found work?" she squeaked.

I nodded, toying with the ends of her hair and resisting the urge to cup her tempting breasts. "Yup. I know you've got a life, and you're busy. I didn't want to be sitting around twiddling my thumbs every day. Can I stay here?"

Delilah bit her lip before she nodded.

"Do you want me here?" I pressed.

She chewed on the inside of her cheek as she stared back

at me. "Of course," she finally whispered as her cheeks turned pink.

My heart gave a thumping beat. I didn't know how to label the way I felt when I was with Delilah. I knew I didn't want to let her and *us* slip away, but I wasn't ready to give my feelings a name.

I did know my desire for her ran deeper than any river on earth, ridiculous as that may sound. When she settled her weight more firmly on my lap, I couldn't resist letting my hands slide down her sides to grip her hips.

Arching my hips slightly, I was gratified when she let out a soft gasp and I felt the heat of her core against my arousal. I eased my grip on her hips, letting one hand slide up to cup a breast. She wore a V-neck T-shirt and a pair of jeans. Nothing special at all. Yet Delilah's unadorned beauty slayed me.

"What made you decide to visit?" she asked with a gasp as I teased my thumb over the tight peak of her nipple.

"I missed you, and I wanted to see you. It's that simple. I called an old friend from college who works at the airport in Asheville. He said he could line up some jobs for me, so I booked a ticket. If you're wondering, I don't mind chasing you across the country."

Delilah leaned forward, pressing an open-mouthed kiss to the side of my neck. That was all it took. "No more talking," she murmured. She nipped my neck and made her way to my mouth.

Kissing Delilah was like diving into a fire. Her mouth was warm and teasing, her tongue tangling with mine. She was a bossy kisser, and I loved it.

I slid my hand through her hair to cup her nape and angled her head to the side, devouring her mouth. Her hands got busy. She shoved my T-shirt up, and I slid my hand over the soft curve of her belly, savoring the feel of her silky skin.

"Alex," she gasped, the word ending with a whimper.

"Yes?" I followed that question with a drag of my tongue along the sensitive skin just above her collarbone.

"I need—"

She ground her hips against me. Next thing I knew, she was fumbling with the buttons on my fly. Reaching between us, I caught her hands with mine. "What do you need?"

"You," she whispered fiercely.

"You got it, sweetheart."

I lifted her off my lap, and she let out a whimper of protest. "Don't worry, just making access easier," I teased.

Our clothes came off in a rush. Then I was sinking back onto the couch, and Delilah was straddling me, her eyes dark on mine. I felt her slick arousal when she rocked her hips over the underside of my cock.

For a few seconds there, I convinced myself I was in control, but I should've known better. There was no such thing as control for me when it came to Delilah. She rose, and I felt the satiny wet kiss of her entrance, then the slow slide as she sheathed me in her silky heat.

Chapter Fourteen

DELILAH

My forehead fell to Alex's. He held me close with one hand gripping my hip and the other wrapped around my waist. My breasts brushed against his chest with every subtle shift of motion. My heart felt as if it were going to burst. Desire was caught in a storm of emotion rushing through me.

The feel of Alex filling and stretching me was intoxicating. I tried to catch my breath, scrambling for purchase in my heart and body, but I couldn't. Sensation caught me in a riptide, and I was towed along in the rush. The pleasure was so intense as it tossed me asunder.

Alex's hand slid up my back in a heated pass, his fingers lacing in my hair. The sting on my scalp was almost a welcome pain. All the while, he lifted me, rocking into me in subtle nudges. The thick, full length of him was a delicious stretch. I savored every stroke as he filled me.

I barely recognized myself, gasping his name again and again with little whimpers escaping while he controlled our pace and kept me from spinning out of control.

"Look at me," he said gruffly.

I'd never considered myself a woman who took orders. It

wasn't as if his order was unreasonable, yet once I was naked with Alex, I did whatever he asked. It was only in the fierce moments like this and only with him that I felt this free.

We were in our own world, one where no rules applied, one where we could be vulnerable. Vulnerable in a way I could never be when I was thinking.

I lifted my head, my eyes meeting his. The look there had my heart kicking hard. Only Alex could steal my breath with nothing more than a look.

"What?" I whispered, my voice frayed with a sharp edge of desire.

"I want to see you when you come."

His words weren't blatantly dirty, but something about the way he said them, something about the look in his eyes that heightened the sensations storming through me. I never thought I could be overtaken. But then, Alex beat every expectation I had about men.

He grabbed my hips with both hands now, lifting slightly. The slow slide up and then the feel of him filling me again was intense, perfect. The angle of his hips against mine pressed against my clit just so, spinning the pressure tighter and tighter inside.

"Alex…"

I could barely keep my eyes open. His face was blurring in my vision. One hand slid up, and his thumb tweaked my nipple. He cupped my cheek, tracing my bottom lip. Another notch of his hips into mine, and I felt the head of his cock press against my cervix. The riptide pulled me under. Pleasure crashed over me, so intense I could hardly breathe. I watched him watching me, the sense of intimacy so deep it was almost frightening.

Alex's hand tightened, his fingers digging into the skin on my hip. His head fell back, the muscles in his neck standing out when he called my name, and I felt the heat of his release filling me.

I collapsed against him, tucking my head into the curve

of his neck, breathing him in and feeling more relaxed than I'd felt in maybe forever. That was what Alex did to me. Here, I thought those two halcyon weeks in Alaska would stand in my memory as forever the best I'd ever feel.

All he had to do was make me miss him and then show up. And now the best ever was pushed to a higher bar.

For the first time, a man fell asleep beside me in my bed. I had rules about that. They were actually pretty easy to keep. You see, I didn't date. I didn't sleep around, either. I occasionally took care of my needs, and that was that.

I didn't trust men. I didn't trust myself not to want to romanticize and tumble into hoping for more. Once again, Alex kicked through the barricades around my heart. I hadn't even hesitated to let him stay. I *wanted* him to stay, almost desperately.

When I woke up during the night to find his hand ghosting across my belly, I rolled toward him, and we made sleepy love in the darkness. I wanted to say it was just sex, but it wasn't. It *so* wasn't.

I fell asleep again wrapped securely in his arms after that. I woke up when I felt the early rays of the sun fall across my face. I came awake sensation by sensation.

The feel of Alex's muscled body spooning me. His arm wrapped around my waist, and his palm splayed on my belly. Even at rest, he was all muscle and strength. I felt entirely secure. I *really* didn't want to get up. Except I had to pee.

I slowly began to move away from Alex, but he tightened his hold on me, moving his hand in a lazy caress over my belly. "Where are you going?"

His voice was gruff and low. Rolling in his arms, I let my eyes coast over his face. His hair was mussed, and his eyes were sleepy. Good grief, the man was handsome even when he had bed head.

"I need to pee," I said bluntly. I felt my cheeks heat slightly, but there was no sense in lying. He was going to hear me get up and go to the bathroom.

When his low chuckle rumbled against my shoulder, little bursts of joy exploded in my heart. God, it felt so good to wake up with him. I'd slept in his arms every single night during my Christmas vacation, but this was different. This was my bed, my world. And my heart.

He dipped his head and dusted his lips across mine before drawing back. "Okay, I'll let you go first," he said magnanimously.

As I rolled out of bed and walked to the bathroom naked, I felt myself swallowing a giggle. A giggle. I did *not* giggle. I just wasn't that kind of girl.

Except when it came to Alex. Alex came with many exceptions to the rule. He was turning out to be a lot like the English language.

I'd never gotten anything lower than an A in English. I pondered whether I could understand the map of my heart in relation to Alex as well as I'd been able to navigate the intricacies of grammar in school.

I was standing at the sink, still completely naked as I washed my hands. I splashed cold water on my face and lifted it, watching the drops of water roll down my cheeks. I felt as if I were living in a dream. As if when I walked out the door, Alex would be gone.

Except I didn't usually sleep naked. I had a favorite soft tank top and a pair of flannel pajama bottoms that I loved. They made me feel cozy and safe. That feeling was nothing compared to the way it felt to fall asleep wrapped in Alex's embrace.

I finally dabbed the towel on my face. *He'll be out there. You're not that crazy.*

There was a sharp knock on the bathroom door. "It's been like two minutes since the toilet flushed, and matters are getting dire out here for my bladder."

This time, I let the giggle break loose from my throat. I swung the door open to find Alex standing there, bare ass naked.

"About damn time," he said with a wide smile as he brushed past me.

He didn't miss the opportunity to reach over and squeeze my bottom. Those little fireworks of joy went off again. I closed the door firmly behind him and had to lean against it to catch my breath and tell myself feeling this happy wasn't smart.

Chapter Fifteen

ALEX

"What the hell are you doing in North Carolina anyway?" Toby asked.

I'd met Toby at flight school. He was a great guy and a good friend. He'd actually come out a few summers and done some flying in Alaska. It was good money, and you could get temp jobs there easily because the work ramped up so much in the summer. When I'd emailed him about a possible trip here, he'd told me he could line up a few jobs with him for me. That had sealed the deal for me coming to see Delilah. Not that I needed to work while I was here, but I knew her schedule wouldn't permit her taking two weeks off, so it kept me busy while she was working.

I tossed a rag stained with all kinds of engine fluids into a bin and turned to wash my hands in the large sink. "I came for a girl."

Toby barked a laugh. "You came all the way to North Carolina for a girl?" His expression could only be described as incredulous.

"Absolutely."

I quickly scrubbed my hands. As I rinsed them under the hot water, Toby asked, "So who is this girl who dragged you all the way across the country?"

"Delilah Carter. She lives in Stolen Hearts Valley."

Turning the water off, I tore a paper towel off the holder and leaned my hips against the sink as I dried my hands.

"That's about forty-five minutes away," Toby observed. "Dude, Alaska to North Carolina is one hell of a commute. How'd you meet her?"

Tossing the paper towel in the trash can by the door, I said, "It's kind of crazy. I met her at camp years ago in Colorado. Never forgot her. Can't say we fell in love, but I had a crazy bad crush back then."

"Y'all stayed in touch all this time?" Toby's brows practically hit his hairline with that question.

"Nah. I sent her a few letters, but she never got them. Turns out, a friend of hers from her hometown moved to Alaska. He's a friend of mine and lives in Willow Brook. Long story short, he and his wife had to cancel a ski trip and gave her the reservation. I found her on the side of a snowy highway. We were both going to the same ski lodge."

"Man, that is wild. I'm not much for believing in fate, but that feels a little bit like it. Are you in love?" he asked.

There went that four letter word. My heart felt like its shelter was being ripped away. Although Delilah meant a lot to me, and I was willing to chase her, I still wasn't ready to label my feelings. I wasn't even sure if we were on the same page yet. My prickly girl was so cynical.

"Yo," Toby said, snapping his fingers in the air.

I realized I'd let the pause go on a little too long. "I don't know. All I know is I missed her, and when you told me you could hook me up with some work here, I got a plane ticket."

"And you're gonna drive back and forth between Asheville and Stolen Hearts Valley every day for two weeks?"

"Well, five days a week," I corrected with a grin.

Toby rolled his eyes. "I'm calling it. You're in love. Now, let's go get lunch."

Chapter Sixteen

ALEX

That evening, I turned off the highway onto the narrower road that led deeper into the Blue Ridge Mountains. The famed blue haze was hanging over the horizon. The fading rays of the sun shot through it in silver, and a watercolor of lavender and pink stained the sky.

It was beautiful here, beautiful enough that a distant corner of my mind considered the idea of moving here to be with Delilah. My thoughts shied away. I wasn't ready to go there.

Delilah had told me she had a lunch shift at the bar and would be getting off around six. I drove straight to Lost Deer Bar. She promised me dinner and good beer when I'd dropped her off earlier.

A few minutes later, I walked into the bar, my eyes scanning the room before I found Delilah. She was sliding a pint of beer across the bar to a customer. She was moving so fast that she barely paused when she snagged the cash and handed over some change while she was already taking an order from another customer.

Her dark hair was pulled into a ponytail, perched high on

her head. It swung as she strode quickly behind the bar. Just
seeing her from across the room had anticipation sizzling in
my veins.

Toby's words rang in my mind. *I'm calling it. You're in
love.*

Maybe I wasn't ready to label how I felt about Delilah,
but I didn't doubt the fierce power of my draw to her. I
weaved my way through the tables and people crowding the
bar, aiming for a corner against the wall. Just as I leaned my
elbows against the bar, Delilah finally saw me.

Her eyes widened slightly as she glanced to the side and
collided with my eyes. A smile curved against her cheek
before she caught herself, schooling it to a slightly milder
version. Oh, Delilah. So guarded, such a challenge. I could
wait.

She finished serving a guy, and I didn't miss the apprecia-
tive gleam in his eyes. Without even trying, Delilah was sexy
as hell. I experienced a twinge of something unfamiliar.
Possessiveness. That was new.

She crossed over to where I was. "Hey," she said simply.

"Hey. When did you say you were done again?"

Delilah's ponytail fell over her shoulder as she angled her
gaze up toward the clock mounted above the door behind
the bar. Her pretty eyes came back to me. "In fifteen
minutes. Do you mind waiting?"

"Absolutely not."

We stared at each other, and my heart twisted in my
chest.

"Do you want something to drink while you wait?"

I couldn't help myself. Reaching across the bar, I caught
the end of her ponytail with one hand to loosely twirl the
ends of it around my fingers. My girl was still a little nervous
around me. She bit her lip.

"Nothing to drink unless I can drink with you," I said
with a quick shake of my head.

Someone called her name. "I gotta go work."

I let her hair slide loose from my hand. "Go work. Don't worry about rushing. I'm here."

Without a word, she spun away, immediately taking a customer's order. Slipping my hips onto a stool, I rested my back against the wall and watched a basketball game on the television mounted behind the bar. This wasn't a sports bar, but practically every bar had a TV.

It wasn't long before Delilah slipped out from behind the bar where the counter had an opening near me. "Ready to go?" she asked.

She had on her fluffy down coat and her purse on her shoulder. I wanted to kiss her, so I did.

Catching one of her hands in mine, I reeled her close between my knees and leaned forward. I meant for it to be a brief kiss, but this was Delilah and me, and we were like a fire always waiting to catch hold. Touching her was like dropping a lit match in dry leaves. *Whoosh*. In a hot second, our tongues were tangling. Delilah gasped into my mouth before she pulled back.

Her eyes were wide, and her cheeks bright pink. There was a low chuckle from beside us, and I glanced over to see her bartender friend, Griffin, grinning from behind the bar. Delilah's ponytail swung when she looked toward him. "Don't you comment," she ordered.

"I'm just glad to see you dating," he replied.

A woman with brown curls spilling everywhere approached with a tall man at her side. "Hey, Delilah. I didn't know you were seeing someone," the woman said.

Delilah didn't even try to hide her sigh. "This is Alex." She looked from me to the woman. "This is Dani and Wade. We grew up together around here."

Wade nodded. "Nice to meet you." His eyes bounced to Dani, the look there expectant.

Dani eyed me, her gaze unabashedly curious. "Hey, Alex. Nice to meet you. You're not from around here."

"Nope. I'm from Alaska. Nice to meet you both."

"Oh, did you meet him when you went on your ski trip?" Dani asked, her voice pitching up an octave as she looked back at Delilah. Before Delilah could even answer, Dani brought her attention back to me. "Wait a sec, do you know Remy?"

"I do. He's a hotshot firefighter in my hometown."

Dani clapped her hands together. "Oh! That's so cool. You'll have to give him a hug for me when you see him."

I chuckled. "Will do."

"That settles it. Y'all have to come out for dinner. Shay will be tickled to meet you. She's Remy's sister," Dani offered.

"Fine by me," I replied, glancing at Delilah to gauge her reaction.

Her cheeks were still pink, but she shrugged. "Sure. Why don't you text me a night that might work?"

After we chatted for a few more minutes with Dani and Wade, Delilah took me over to Lost Deer Winery for dinner. "This is a sort of fancy restaurant," she commented as we walked in. "It's owned by the same people who own the bar where I work."

The winery restaurant was nice. It was a large space with tall ceilings and windows offering a view of Stolen Hearts Valley. We were seated at a table by the windows, and Delilah asked me what I wanted to drink.

"I'll take whatever you suggest."

"Have you ever had mead?"

"Once or twice. There's a brewery in Diamond Creek where the ski lodge is. I don't think I took you there. Anyway, they sell mead."

Our waiter came, and Delilah ordered two meads for us to try. The waiter reeled off the specials, and we ordered. As he walked away, I took a moment to look at Delilah. She had taken her hair down on the drive over, and it spilled around her shoulders. I loved her hair, and it tended to bring inappropriate thoughts to mind. For example, a memory of one of our nights over the holidays when I had her hair wrapped around my fist, and her hands were curled on the headboard.

So not the time to go there. I adjusted my jeans. "So I'm supposed to give Shay a hug for Remy. Do you mind having dinner with her? I assume they're your friends since they gave you their ski trip."

Delilah nodded. "They are. I went to high school with Shay. Remy's a good guy."

"The best. So tell me about your family," I said conversationally. She was still reticent about her family, but since I was here in Stolen Hearts Valley, it seemed natural to ask about them.

Delilah rubbed her thumb and forefinger together and gave a light shrug. "My parents live here. I'm not on the best terms with my dad, but my mom and I are a little better."

This was the downside to the temporary footing of my relationship with Delilah so far. We met at camp years ago. Then we met again during a ski vacation over the holidays. Nothing about those two episodes were like our normal lives. Except, in my case, she met my sister and my best friend.

"I didn't have the greatest childhood, Alex." This came out almost forcefully, her eyes bouncing away quickly as she looked down.

Ah, perhaps a clue to my girl.

"Lots of people didn't have the best childhood. I'm just curious. I want to know you," I said, keeping my tone mellow.

Delilah's eyes bounced to mine and away again. A look of relief crossed her face when the waiter arrived with our drinks.

I took a swallow a moment later. "Wow, that's good," I said as I lowered my glass to the table.

Delilah smiled. "Yeah, I never knew I liked mead until I tried it. It's yummy."

"Tell me about your life," I pressed.

Delilah angled her head to the side, pinching the bridge of her nose when she let out a sigh. "Okay. My dad's an alcoholic. But before you go thinking the worst, he didn't beat us up or anything. He just couldn't hold a job to save his life. That's why I never got your letter. They got evicted while I was away at camp. I don't think we ever lived in one place for more than a few months. I could see it was the alcohol owning him, but it still sucked."

I wanted to wrap Delilah in my arms. As she spoke, she lifted her chin, and that steely look I'd come to know entered her gaze.

"What about your mom?"

A rueful smile curled her lips. "She did her best under not very good circumstances. I always wanted her to leave him. If it hadn't been for her having a job the whole time, we wouldn't even have had food on the table sometimes."

"What does she do?"

"Nothing amazing. My grandmother ran a greenhouse and landscaping business on her property, and my mom helped her with it. That's where my parents live now. My dad could've helped with the landscaping side of things, but he was too inconsistent. So that's it. That's my parents and my childhood."

Delilah's mouth twisted with her words, and she looked away quickly, making a show of looking out the windows. I hadn't even realized I reached for her hand until my fingers curled over hers, and I felt how cold she was. She jerked slightly, whipping her head back in my direction.

"You're cold," I commented.

"My hands are usually cold in the winter."

I supposed that was true, but I could feel the slight tremor running through her. If I hadn't figured it out yet, her family was obviously a sore spot for her.

"I'm sorry your childhood kind of sucked," I finally said, knowing blunt and direct usually was Delilah's preference.

She shrugged. "It's okay. Life isn't fair, right? Your family sounds nice. I like Holly."

My family *was* pretty awesome, and I knew I was blessed. Even though my twin sister could drive me crazy, I loved her. She'd stop traffic for me, just as I would do the same for her.

"Maybe I can talk you into coming to visit Willow Brook. I think you'd like it."

"Maybe," Delilah replied, her tone carefully neutral.

Delilah wasn't one to let herself get hopeful. Her doubts were practically plastered like billboards on her face, so I let it go.

Our food came, and it was delicious. We went home that night. Once again, we had the kind of sex that made me forget everything else.

Chapter Seventeen

DELILAH

"I know we haven't met before, but I'm going to hug you," Shay said as she approached Alex.

We were having the dinner Dani suggested, except Dani was working, so it was me and Alex with Shay and Jackson. Dani easily rivaled me with her tendency to work all the time. With her fiancé, Wade, on call as a first responder tonight, he had passed on dinner as well.

Alex shrugged affably. He was an easygoing guy and didn't mind being hugged by a stranger.

Shay was Remy's little sister. We'd gone to high school together, and Remy had been a few years ahead of us. Shay was engaged to Jackson Stone now. As far as I could tell, they were ridiculously in love. Like the fairy tale kind of love.

"You must be Jackson," Alex said after Shay stepped back from hugging him.

Jackson threw his head back with a laugh, and they gave each other a backslapping hug. "Remy's one of my best buddies. You can tell him that hug was for him."

Alex grinned. "You got it, man." He glanced around the

lodge restaurant. "Nice place here. Remy told me you own it."

"Let's get a table," Jackson said, gesturing for us to follow him.

I'd been to this restaurant before but not often because it wasn't cheap. Seeing as Jackson did own it, we had a great table by the windows looking out over the valley. The sun was setting, casting the smoky blue over the mountains with shades of silver and lavender.

"My sister and I inherited the farm from our parents," Jackson began once we were seated. "It hasn't been a working farm for a while, and my dad started up an animal rescue before he passed away. We've got a vet clinic in the rescue over in the original part of the farm. This barn is for the guests, and we have lodging upstairs."

"Y'all have made an amazing place," I said, meaning every word.

"Thanks, Delilah," Jackson said, dipping his head in a nod. "We're proud of it."

"The Lost Deer owners sure love it. They get to send their wine and beer over here," I replied, referring to the owners of the bar where I worked.

"It's a mutually beneficial relationship," Jackson offered.

A waiter came by, and Dani waved as she hurried by at one point. We had a relaxing dinner, and I actually enjoyed it. I was so busy that I rarely had extra time to socialize with friends. I saw Shay at the bar when she came by, along with most of my friends, but I was always working.

"How've you been, Delilah?" Shay said as dinner moved along, her green eyes twinkling with her smile. "Seems like that Alaska trip turned out to be a boon."

I felt my cheeks go pink, and I shrugged. Shay cast a quick look in Alex's direction, but he was busy talking to Jackson about his job as an airplane mechanic.

"He seems nice," she said, keeping her voice low.

"He really is," I said, meaning it down to my bones.

Having Alex at my side was such a small thing, but it was a strange experience for me. I didn't date. I just didn't count on thinking anyone would want to go the long haul with me. More accurately, I didn't want to let myself count on anyone or anything. Especially not a man.

"He flew all the way here for you, so he must like you."

My cheeks got hotter. Shay smiled. "I just want you to be happy."

Jackson asked her something then, and she let the topic drop.

It was another night that ended with me tangled up with Alex. That man was magic, and I was going to deeply miss falling asleep wrapped in his arms.

Chapter Eighteen

DELILAH

"Do you want to meet my parents?"

Alex was chewing on a bite of a bagel, and he nodded while he continued chewing.

"I'm not sure it can happen since you're leaving tomorrow, but if you visit again, I'll make sure to try to introduce you." I didn't say the silent part out loud—that I hadn't even attempted to coordinate a way for him to meet them. Although I felt a sting of shame about that, it wasn't as if I saw my parents on a weekly basis. Maybe once a month or so. Alex was gracious enough to let it rest. Whether he spoke it aloud, I sensed he understood how touchy the topic of my parents was and didn't push. That rankled slightly because it only illuminated how much he understood me. *That* was what terrified me.

Nobody ever wanted to meet my parents. But then I'd never really dated anyone long enough that they might ask. It wasn't as if Alex and I were *dating*, though. We were having these strange interludes that didn't feel like my real life. Except this interlude sort of did.

Alex was here. In my world. He worked in Asheville

while I bounced between my shifts at the bar and cramming in my nursing school classes at night. He was even gracious about that. He would watch TV and put my legs over his lap while I tapped away on my laptop.

I loved it. Too often, I caught myself imagining us being a *real* couple. That was freaking crazy. Having experienced disappointment and disruption too many times in my childhood, I'd learned to set the bar of expectations low.

It would be enough just to have a stable income and an apartment I liked. It would be enough to be able to make my own decisions about where I lived and what I did. It would be enough to stay single even if I wanted more because then I didn't have to worry about anyone ever letting me down. It would be amazing not to live in a household with an alcoholic.

Almost every day, I caught myself wanting to tell Alex about my father being sick and dying. For reasons I didn't understand, not even a little, I struggled to tell him. It seemed so personal.

Um, getting naked with him and having wildly intimate sex every night is pretty personal. My snide and always ready to be critical voice chimed in.

Tonight was our last night together before Alex flew back to Alaska. I hated how much I was going to miss him. Now, it was going to be worse than before. I had a taste of him in my daily life, and I loved every minute of it.

"Could you practice being just a little bit of an asshole?" I asked.

Alex looked over from where he was changing the channel on the television. My calves rested on his lap. He was absentmindedly rubbing one of my feet, which he did often. Considering that being a bartender meant I spent hours on my feet, it was a special slice of heaven.

"Practice being an asshole?" One of his dark brows rose in a slash.

"Yeah, like leaving a towel on the floor or leaving your

dishes on the coffee table." I gestured toward the empty plate currently sitting there. I knew he would carry it into the kitchen, rinse it, and put it in the dishwasher the next time he got up from the couch. We'd gotten takeout tonight from a Thai place in Asheville. Or rather, Alex had picked it up and brought it home. He knew I had one of my online classes tonight, and he hadn't even complained about that even though it was his last night here.

"Come to think of it, you could complain that I had a class tonight." I closed my laptop and shifted it onto the coffee table.

"School is important to you. I knew I'd be eating and relaxing and packing, so that's what I did. No biggie," he said easily.

He studied me quietly, getting that piercing look in his eyes that he had sometimes. It made me want to squirm a little bit. A part of me savored how well Alex seemed to understand me. Another part of me, a pretty loud and opinionated part of me, wanted to run for my life when I felt his understanding.

I'd spent my whole childhood waiting until I could be an adult and didn't have to count on anyone, yet I found myself wishing I could count on Alex. But I lived here, and he lived over four thousand miles away. He had a life there and a family—the kind of family anyone would want.

My mother's comment—*Don't be afraid to take a chance*—dashed through my thoughts, so surprising, it was like a nude streaker at a public event.

Even thinking about moving to Alaska scared me because then that meant I was hanging my hopes on something. Or more specifically, on someone—Alex.

"If you want to know annoying things about me, just call Holly. She'll give you a long list." He offered a mischievous grin with that comment.

I laughed. "I bet she would, but she's your sister. She's biased, both good and bad."

"I checked prices. I can get you a ticket to Alaska over your break from school. It's about six weeks out, right?" Alex asked, his tone carefully light.

See, that was exactly what I meant about him. He understood me. He knew this would make me feel squirrely, so he offered it up as casually as if he was mentioning the weather.

I swallowed, willing my heart to calm down. My heart was having none of that and rioted in my chest. It was as if a flock of small birds in a tree took flight together, all calling at once and filling the sky with a cacophony of sounds.

"I don't know," I said, nervously catching the edge of the throw blanket draped on the back of the couch and rubbing the soft fabric between my fingers.

"I know you don't know. Think about it. Please. I know you've seen Alaska, but I'd like you to come to Willow Brook. You can see where I grew up and see Holly. She'd love that. Just let me know by next week, okay?"

"Okay." I was relieved he didn't press further, yet on the heels of my relief came a twinge of disappointment. See, I wanted him to beg. Good Lord. It wasn't enough that he was offering to buy me a freaking plane ticket. I knew they weren't cheap.

After Alex did exactly as I knew he would and took his plate to the dishwasher, he even rinsed the dishes I'd left in the sink. When I was coming out of the bathroom, I saw him turning the dishwasher on. Crossing the kitchen, I leaned my hips against the counter and curled my hands on the edges. "See, you don't know how to be an asshole."

Alex turned. Inside of a nanosecond, his eyes darkened, and heat coiled inside me, suffusing me from head to toe. Moving quickly to me, Alex was lifting me and sliding my hips on the counter before I even realized what was happening.

Stepping between my knees, he tugged me against his arousal. I could feel the thick, hard length of him pressing against me. I became acutely aware of the slick heat at the apex of my thighs. I was already wet. Alex made me feel like a ridiculously needy girl. Aside from the muddled confusion I felt at the depth of how much emotion he elicited, I felt even more vulnerable at the shocking force of my desire for him.

The only relief in all of my internal tumult was that I could simply forget myself the moment he kissed me. Thank goodness for that. Before Alex, I was used to having my brain halfway on whenever I had sex.

I wasn't complaining about other men specifically. It's just that no one else captured my attention thoroughly enough to wash my thoughts away in the current of passion. I found myself wondering about homework assignments for school, or trying to remember my work schedule, or worrying about bills. The mundane could always puncture what was supposed to be a moment of desire. Except with Alex.

I looked into his dark chocolate eyes, and my heart gave a sweet twist in my chest. My breath hitched when I tried to get some air. I could hear the rush of blood in my ears with the thundering beat of my heart as Alex stared at me. It was hard to look at him because tomorrow he was leaving.

He saved me from myself by dipping his head and pressing a hot, open kiss on my neck, just behind my ear. That spot was so sensitive it sent a shiver through my entire body, my skin prickling with goose bumps and liquid need spreading like lava through my veins.

"Alex." I gasped when he trailed his tongue along my collarbone.

"Yeah, sweetheart?"

His hand snuck under my shirt, cupping one of my breasts and teasing the already hard nipple to an aching peak. "I need..." I couldn't even cling to a train of thought, and my words ended on a moan. What did I need? I had no idea. I just *needed*.

"I've got you," he murmured.

He did have me—body, heart, and soul.

Our clothes came off in a rush, and somehow, we stumbled into the bedroom. Something about Alex saying he needed to take his time.

I was naked and restless, my skin dewy. I shifted my legs, feeling the juices of my arousal on the inside of my thighs.

Alex had kicked his jeans off and was standing at the foot of the bed. His hungry gaze swept up and down my body. I literally felt it on my skin, little licks of fire everywhere his eyes landed.

The mattress dipped under his weight when he brought one knee down. Curling his hands around my ankles, he moved his touch upward in a smooth, sure path as he pushed my knees apart. He muttered something. I didn't even know what it was, but I felt it, dirty and sweet at once. He dropped hot kisses on the insides of my thighs, and my hips rocked into his touch the moment his fingers trailed lightly through my folds.

"So wet," he murmured.

"Alex," I pleaded.

He gave me what I needed, sinking two fingers into my channel. When he drew them out, I whimpered in protest. But then he licked the very core of me, and I let out a long moan.

My fingers tangled in his hair, and I gripped the sheets with my other hand. Alex made love to me with his mouth, taking me to the edge and pulling me back again and again. It felt as if I was made of pleasure, every cell tightening and tightening, begging for more.

Finally, he rose, just when I cried his name again. "Sweetheart, I want you to come all over my cock," he said.

Pulling my eyes open, I looked up to see him fisting his cock. He dragged the head back and forth through my folds, and each time the thick crown teased over my clit, I almost toppled over the edge.

"Alex," I begged. I had no shame, and this man made me plead like no other.

"Right here, sweetheart," he murmured, just before notching his cock at my entrance and sinking inside in one slow slide.

Chapter Nineteen

ALEX

Delilah's hot, silky core sheathed me. I nearly came instantly, but I gritted my teeth and clung to my control. Her dark hair was a tangled mess on the pillows, and her eyes held mine.

I eased over her, resting on one elbow as I brushed her hair away from her face. Her legs curled around my hips, and she arched against me. "Alex."

My heart felt cracked open. I loved it when she said my name. The only time she was this unguarded was when we were having sex. We were so, so good together.

Drawing back, I felt her begin to ripple around my cock when I sank inside her again, her channel clenching me tightly. One more slow slide and her entire body trembled as she cried out.

The heaviness in my balls tightened, and everything sizzled before my release slammed through me. I came so hard I collapsed against her. I practically saw stars. When the edges of my vision cleared, I rolled over, bringing her on top of me. I felt the rapid beat of her heart thundering along with mine.

I didn't want to let her go. I didn't want to leave tomorrow. I held her and stroked my hands through her hair, knowing if I pushed too hard or too fast with her, it would ruin everything.

Chapter Twenty

DELILAH

I turned along the road that led to the airport, feeling a little sick inside. I'd tried to make this morning normal. We had coffee, and I made omelets for breakfast. Alex insisted on helping me clean up, which annoyed me.

He'd returned his rental car two days ago after I insisted I could take him to the airport. I was now regretting that choice because I felt like a foolish girl. I was going to miss him, and this impending goodbye was bearing down on me at warp speed. I wasn't ready to take the hit.

As I got farther down the road to the airport, it felt as if the signs were even pressuring me. I had to decide between short-term parking and just dropping him off at the curb. The decision felt ominous. I didn't know which choice to make. If Alex hadn't been in the car with me, I'd probably have driven a few loops while my thoughts went to war with themselves.

But it was as if he could read my mind as he reached across the console, sliding his hand onto my thigh. "If it's easier for you, you can drop me off at the curb. You can't go to the gate anyway."

All of the sudden, I knew the answer. "I'm walking you to security," I said.

His eyes widened in surprise, and I smiled. I liked surprising Alex, even over something this small.

We didn't talk while Alex got his bag, and we walked together through the parking garage into the airport. I waited while he checked in. Of course, he didn't check a bag. The man had packed enough clothes in his backpack for two weeks, which I thought was pretty remarkable.

He reached for my hand as we began to walk toward security. I looked around at all the other people hurrying past us through the airport and wondered if anyone else's heart was breaking like mine.

When we got to the area before he would get in line to go through security, he stopped and turned to face me. He let his backpack slide off his shoulder and rest on the floor by his feet.

Capturing both of my hands in his, he searched my face quietly. "Did you decide about coming out to visit over your break? You can tell me next week if you'd rather think about it some more."

I had decided, but I was such a chickenshit that I'd been afraid to tell him. I swallowed through the tightness in my throat and nodded.

"Is that a 'yes, you're coming' or a more general 'yes, you decided'?" A smile teased at the corners of his mouth.

"Yes," I whispered. "I'll come. Though I'm not sure how I feel about you getting my tickets."

I could only bear to look at him for so long, so I dropped my eyes to the floor and stared at our feet. I'd worn a pair of tennis shoes, as he had, after he commented he needed something comfortable since he had to be on the plane for over twelve hours.

He released one of my hands, then lifted my chin lightly with his knuckles. I looked in his eyes again and hoped he couldn't tell I was about to cry. The sheer joy contained in his gaze set my heart to pounding crazy hard.

"Awesome. As soon as I land, I'll take care of the tickets and send you an email. Okay?"

"Okay." I couldn't seem to speak above a whisper.

There was an announcement over the airport speaker, and a family hurried by us, one of the kids dropping a bag. A woman scooped it up, and they kept moving.

"I should go," he said.

"Okay." My vocabulary had deteriorated, it seemed.

Alex wrapped me in his arms, giving me one of those hugs that made me feel so secure. I burrowed my head into his chest and breathed in his scent, hoping I wouldn't forget it.

Chapter Twenty-One
ALEX

April

"When did you say Delilah would be here?" Holly asked.

I glanced at my watch as if the time itself would tell me when. Holly, being my ever-obnoxious sister and always quick to notice every detail, added, "You don't have a fancy watch with a calendar on it, dude."

Nate let out a chuckle from across the table. Glancing back and forth between them, I replied, "I know. Three more weeks. That's when her break from school is."

"How is nursing school going for her?" Holly asked, her eyes bright and curious.

"Good, I think. I know when I was visiting, she did homework every night and then online classes three times a week."

"Do you know how far into her program she is?" Holly chimed in with another question.

"Uh, no," I replied. "Is that something I should know?"

Holly pursed her lips. "Yes, dummy. You flew all the way

across the country to spend two weeks with her and paid for her to come back here for another week. You should know everything."

"About her nursing school program?" I was genuinely mystified.

Nate, being the best friend he was, leaned his elbows on the table with a sympathetic gaze. We were at Wildlands Bar, a favorite local bar and restaurant. I had run into Nate at his plane hangar when I went out to take care of a few repairs on another plane, and he'd suggested we come by here for dinner. Of course, Holly met us here as well.

"Holly thinks you're in love. By extension, that means knowing absolutely everything about a woman, no matter how irrelevant it is to your relationship," Nate offered with a grin.

"Does Nate know everything about your work?" I asked, looking at my twin sister.

"Sure," she said sharply.

When I flicked my eyes toward Nate, I knew he didn't. "I bet he doesn't even know your schedule tomorrow. Or next week, for that matter. And I bet you don't know his."

Holly bit her lip and then stuck her tongue out at me.

"Nice, that's mature. I'll talk to Delilah and find out where she's at in her nursing school program."

"If she moves here, she can do her nursing internship at the hospital," Holly said excitedly, actually rubbing her hands together.

"I don't know if we're at the moving-across-the-country stage yet."

Just hearing Holly's suggestion had my heart giving a funny little tumble in my chest. Even if I lived where Delilah did, whether that was here or North Carolina or somewhere else, I knew I'd have to play my cards just so to convince her we could have something real. She took cynical and guarded to new levels.

Holly gave me another pointed look. "Well, Delilah sure

as hell isn't gonna consider it if you're all doubtful. I hear all these amazing things about people who meet long distance and fall in love. They learn all the stuff about each other before they actually live together. I think it's a really cool way to get to know someone. You should take advantage of the distance."

"Says the girl who married my best friend from childhood. You two have known each other since before you can even remember," I muttered.

Nate chuckled and leaned back in the booth, resting his arm across Holly's shoulders. "He's got a point."

Holly shook her head and let out a little harrumph. "Well, it's not like he's known Delilah since they were kids. I'm just trying to talk about his situation, not mine."

———

"What did you say?"

Delilah was silent on the other end. Her sigh filtered through the phone line, and I sensed she was annoyed. Meanwhile, I was shocked and confused.

"My father is sick."

I remembered how she had carefully avoided introducing me to her parents, even after I had asked her about it. I was becoming painfully aware of how little I knew about Delilah. It wasn't just the status of nursing school. It was everything.

"How sick?" I asked.

"He's dying," she whispered.

"I'm sorry," I said, my voice coming out rough. "Why didn't you tell me sooner?"

Trying to imagine her face, I pictured her eyes looking at me suspiciously because I knew she didn't like it when I asked personal questions. Just now, I was starting to feel like she was never going to let this thing with us be anything more than at arm's length. In our case, there was almost an entire continent between us.

"I don't know. I don't talk a lot about my personal life. With anyone. I'm not used to it. When I was growing up, I couldn't invite friends over because of how things were at home, so it's a habit not to talk about it," she explained.

"When did you find out he was sick?" I asked gently.

"Not long after I got back from my trip over the holidays."

I could hear the defensiveness in her tone. I reminded myself that it wasn't helpful for me to get upset with her for not telling me this. It wasn't the details that I was upset about. It was realizing just how much she kept herself at bay from me.

"Is this why you didn't want me to meet your parents when I was visiting?"

"I guess. Alex, don't take this personally. My mom and I talk, but I haven't been close to my dad. Ever. He has colon cancer, and it's bad. My mother says the doctors say he's only got a few months left."

"I'm so sorry, Delilah." My words felt like they fell far too short of what she needed. I wanted to hold her.

Because I came from a loving family, it was hard for me to imagine how she must feel. I wanted to be able to see her face. "Can we switch to a video call?" I asked, my mouth running ahead of my thoughts.

Delilah was quiet for a few beats, the silence heavy through the phone line. "Okay," she finally whispered.

"I'm hanging up, and I'll call right back."

As soon as I hit the button to end the call, I realized she might not answer again. I tapped to open the video call screen, hit her number, and waited. My breath came out in a whoosh when she answered. She wasn't really a fan of video calls. I tried to get her to do them every night, and she was always squirrely about it.

I sensed I knew exactly why. There was nowhere to look but at each other.

"Hey," I said softly when I saw her face. Lines of tension bracketed her eyes and mouth, and she looked tired.

"Fuck," Delilah began, nervously brushing her hair away from her face. "You're so good and so nice, and I'm just not used to having anyone even ask. I hope you don't take it the wrong way that I didn't mention what was going on with my father sooner."

Crazy as it sounded, her worry made me a little happy. Not because I wanted her to be worried. No, that scored my heart with sharp claws, and I hated that she was thousands of miles away from me. Yet her worry meant she understood this mattered to me, that *she* mattered to me. That felt incredible, like a monumental achievement.

"It's okay," I said. "I'm really sorry about your dad. Is there anything I can do to help?"

Delilah's pretty mouth twisted as she shook her head. "No. It's just weird. I went over there yesterday when my mom said he might be awake. He was, but he was pretty out of it. They're already giving him hospice care. He's been an alcoholic his whole life, and now he's doped up on pain medicine. I don't mind. I want him to be comfortable."

"I'm glad he's comfortable, even if he's out of it." I paused, trying to gather my thoughts. I forged ahead even though I wasn't even clear on what I was trying to express. "I can't say I know or understand what you went through growing up because my childhood wasn't like that. I do know it would be hard not to have parents I felt like I could turn to, and I'm sorry you didn't have that. If there's anything I could give you, I want to give you a place where you feel like you belong."

Delilah's gaze searched mine through the phone screen. I thought I saw a little flicker of something in her eyes, but I wasn't sure.

"I'd love that," she finally said. "Tell me about your family."

"Well, you know Holly. She's my twin sister. It was just me and her. My father is a pilot, like me."

"You're a pilot too?" Delilah interjected.

"Yeah, I hadn't mentioned that? My job is an airplane mechanic, but I can also fly." She smiled, and damn, that felt good. "So yeah, like Nate. You remember him from Christmas, right?" At Delilah's nod, I continued, "My dad was a bush pilot, and he flew all over Alaska before he retired. My mom is a nurse. She's retired. Well, not one hundred percent. She fills in when they need help in a pinch at the hospital. Before you get here for your visit, you should know Holly wants you to do your internship in Willow Brook at the hospital. She also gave me a lecture because apparently, I'm supposed to know everything about your nursing program."

Delilah laughed. "How is Holly? Also, next year is when I'm scheduled to do my internship."

I didn't miss that she completely avoided addressing Holly's proposal that she do it in Willow Brook, but I decided to leave that alone for now. "Holly's just fine. My parents are still together, and they still live in the house where I grew up. Whether you want to or not, I'm not sure I can avoid having you meet them when you come to visit. Willow Brook is a small town, and Holly's already told them you're coming. Sorry about that."

She shrugged lightly. "It's okay. I already met Holly. If I can handle her, I can probably handle your parents, right?"

"You can handle anyone, Delilah."

Her cheeks went pink. "I have a class in five minutes. I should go because I need to get some dinner heated up before I start."

"Got it. Thanks for telling me about your dad."

Delilah nodded. She pressed two fingers to her lips and blew a kiss to me.

Chapter Twenty-Two

DELILAH

"Hey, Dee," my father said, using a nickname only he ever used with me.

When I was little, I hated it because it represented a laziness to me, like everything he did. Just as he couldn't be bothered to keep a job, not to drink, and just generally do life, he also couldn't manage to say my full name. Not that anything was wrong with that particular nickname. It's just no one else used it with me.

Right now, though, my stomach felt funny. It had that hollow feeling you get when an elevator moves suddenly, or when you're riding a roller coaster and descending abruptly. Because he was the only one who ever called me by that nickname, there would only be a limited number of times I would hear myself addressed that way again.

Sadness swamped me, and I actually had to close my eyes for a minute as I sat down in the chair by his bed. Opening them, I saw my father's eyes were closed where he lay on the bed. He looked frail. His arms were thin, and his skin was papery. His color was faded. It was almost as if the light of life inside him was slowly dimming. Which, I supposed, it was.

"Hey, Dad. How are you feeling?"

"Like shit," he replied with a chuckle as he opened his eyes.

That was one thing I could say I'd learned from my dad. He was always blunt and forthright. Even about his tendency to be a "falling down drunk." His words, not mine.

I reached out to squeeze his hand, startled at how weak his grip was when he gave me a squeeze in return. Drawing my hand back, I laced my fingers together and rested them over one of my knees. I bounced my foot restlessly just as I did whenever I was anxious.

My father rolled his head away to look out the window beside the bed. It was raining today, rather fitting for my mood. I felt as melancholy and gray inside as the sky was outside, and the rain represented my unshed tears. I almost jumped in my chair when he spoke, his voice raspy.

"I know I wasn't the best father. I hope you know I loved you, still do. I went to an AA meeting last week."

I was relieved he was looking out the window because my mouth dropped open in shock. He caught me as he turned back and smiled softly. "It's all right. You can be as shocked as you want. I've been ragging on AA my whole life. I went because I guess I wanted to figure out one thing before I died."

"What's that, Dad?"

I felt like a little girl again. As if I was peering around the corner and waiting to see my dad do what I always wished he would do—pull himself together.

"Well, I can't get sober, and I don't suppose I have time to do the steps about mending things. But I can tell you I'm sorry that I let alcohol steal my life and your childhood."

I didn't realize I was crying until I felt the path of a tear roll down my cheek, cooling in the air. My dad reached over slowly to the nightstand and handed me a box of tissues. I started laughing. After blowing my nose and dabbing at my eyes, I balled the tissue in my hand.

"It's not worth much now, but I'm sorry," my father added.

His blue eyes held mine as I studied his face. He had the skin of an alcoholic. Under the surface of his pale skin was a visible map of broken blood vessels.

"It's okay, Dad. I'm sorry you're sick."

"That's okay too. Hell, for years, I tried to get pain pills. Never could, but I had to go to the doctor so that made it harder. Now, I'm all dosed up," he offered with a chuckle.

"I want you to be comfortable. Are you sure you're okay that I'm gonna be gone for a week?"

"Course I am. Your mama says you met a guy. Please tell me he doesn't have a problem with drinking."

"He doesn't." I shook my head, kind of hard, and my chest felt really tight.

"Tell me about him."

In a conversation I absolutely *never* expected to have, I sat there in the chair beside my father's bed and told him almost everything I knew about Alex—how we met at camp, the ski trip, Alex buying me a ticket. Well, except for the sex. I left that out.

I talked until my father's eyes fell closed, and he was breathing in the soft, easy rhythm of sleep.

Chapter Twenty-Three

DELILAH

Late April

Once again, I found myself looking out the window of the plane, marveling at the sight of the jagged mountain range below, the snow-covered peaks a stark contrast against the blue sky. The surface of the ocean ruffled under the wind as the plane lowered when we approached Anchorage.

The minute we landed, my pulse started humming. As soon as we got the clear to turn on our personal devices, I turned mine on. It vibrated immediately with a text from Alex.

Alex: *Waiting just outside the security area.* I got the emoticon with a giant smile at the end of his one sentence text.

My heart was going insane, bouncing around in my chest with excitement. Minutes later, I was walking with a cluster of people. When we turned a corner in the hallway, I saw Alex standing just beyond the glass doors that separated this part of the airport with the non-secured section.

His eyes were searching through the group of people. I felt a low tug in my belly when his gaze landed on me. My heart thudded hard, and my breath hitched in my throat. He smiled, and I felt my own lips curling up in return.

I felt like such a foolish girl when it came to Alex. Beyond excited, I really wanted to squeal and run through the crowd. As it was, I had to wait because a little girl dropped her bag in front of me, and I almost tripped over it. She started crying, and then I found myself helping her mother who was also holding the hand of another toddler on the other side.

Once the little girl stopped crying and they were moving forward, I looked up to see Alex still waiting. I didn't even know what to think about just how cynical I was. For a second, I had actually wondered if he'd left. I mean, that was crazy. He was here to pick me up. He'd bought my plane ticket. Why would he leave?

It's just I wasn't used to anyone going out of their way for me like that. I finally stepped through the doors that said I couldn't turn around. If my point of no return meant getting wrapped in Alex's arms, that was a pretty good deal.

He didn't even speak. He simply stepped to me and pulled me into his strong embrace. I could feel him head to toe, and I took a deep breath, letting out a shaky sigh as I buried my face in his chest. He smelled so good.

After a minute, I lifted my head as he stroked his hand in easy passes up and down my back. I found his brown eyes waiting for me.

"Hey," he said.

"Hey," I returned.

We stared at each other for a long moment, and I felt a laugh bubbling up. When it slipped out, he chuckled before asking, "What's so funny?"

"I don't know."

I actually didn't know. I thought my laughter was simply

because of my nerves. It was a good kind of anticipation, but I was still nervous.

When someone jostled me from behind, Alex reached for my bag, which I hadn't even noticed I'd dropped. My small rolling suitcase had fallen to the floor, its handle stretching out across the tile. Leaning over, he picked it up, turning and keeping an arm firmly around my waist.

"You ready to go?" he asked.

"Of course. Unless you want to hang out in the airport."

We began walking side by side, and I looked up to see his cheek curving with a smile. "I wouldn't mind hanging out in the airport as long as you're here. Did you have any checked bags?"

I shook my head. "Nope. I hate dealing with the baggage claim, plus it's expensive now. You have to pay to check even one bag."

"I get it. Whether or not I can afford to cover the bags, it's kind of the principle of it. I hate paying for it. Glad you brought your down coat," he observed as he glanced down at me.

I had my coat folded over my arm. "I wasn't sure how cold it would be. I checked the weather, and it looks like it's going to be warmer during the day, but the nights look cold."

Alex nodded. "Mud season's about here," he explained. "It's not the prettiest time of year here. I'd like you to come again in the summer so you can see the fireweed."

I didn't know how to reply because that meant planning for the future. It had taken so much courage just to take this trip. I wasn't sure I was ready for more. My plane had landed late, and it was dark when we stepped outside at the airport. Alex never broke stride and never released his arm from around my waist. His palm curled over the edge of my pelvis, and I loved it. I loved him holding me close.

Although I knew we were in Alaska, it was funny how all airports felt the same. We stepped out of a revolving door onto a sidewalk where taxis and car services were lined up to pick up the people spilling out of the airport.

My breath misted in the air. I was chilly enough that I wanted to put my jacket on. I didn't, though, because that meant stepping away from Alex as we walked into the parking garage. When we reached his truck, I glanced at him. "Did you leave it running this whole time?"

He chuckled. "Of course not. I have a remote starter. I started it as soon as I saw you come through the gate. It's cold out, so I wanted it to be warm for you."

I grinned as I climbed in. "This is the same truck you picked me up in when I ran off the road before Christmas," I said as I buckled my seat belt.

Alex, because he had manners, had put my suitcase away and insisted I put my jacket on. He glanced sideways as he buckled his own seat belt. "Of course it is. I don't have two vehicles. Just this one."

My God, I was ridiculous around him. Joy fizzed through me as I smiled back at him.

We were quiet as he drove out of the parking garage and paid the fee. When I offered to pay it, he ignored me, and a sense of insecurity stole through me. I spent most of my life not having enough—not enough money, not enough clothes, not enough anything. He'd insisted on paying for my plane ticket, and I was willing to bet he was going to try to cover everything while I was here.

"Please let me pay for something." My words slipped out before I could catch myself.

One of Alex's hands rested over the steering wheel as he glanced toward me. "I'm hosting you," he said as if that explained everything.

"But you flew yourself to North Carolina," I protested, not sure why I was even bringing this up. It made me feel a little twitchy inside.

The stoplight where we'd been waiting turned green. As he drove ahead, I fell quiet, telling myself to shut up about it. I didn't have a ton of money. Every extra penny I had went into covering my nursing school tuition.

"I don't want to argue about money," Alex finally said as he took a ramp onto a highway.

"I don't either," I said softly.

Because I was looking out the window and trying not to be irrationally upset, I didn't realize he was reaching for my hand until he caught it in his, bringing it over to his lap, his grip warm and firm.

"Stop worrying. I can practically see the wheels spinning in your brain," he said.

I could hear the smile in his voice, and the tension that had started to bundle in my chest loosened slightly. "Okay, I'll try. How far away are we from Willow Brook?" I asked, figuring I might as well change the subject so I could distract myself from worrying.

"Forty-five minutes, give or take a little. In just a few minutes, we'll be out of the lights from the city, and you can enjoy the view."

"It's dark," I stated the obvious. "How am I going to see the view?"

Alex chuckled and gave my hand a squeeze where his fingers were laced with mine. "The moon is out tonight, and it's clear. I promise there's a view."

As he predicted, a few minutes later, I looked out the window and saw the silhouette of a mountain range. Bright stars glittered through the darkness. When I looked at the other side, the moonlight was cast across the water. Its surface rippled under the pearly illumination.

"Is Willow Brook on the ocean?" I asked.

"It's close," Alex replied. "There's a big lake in town, and the ocean's about twenty minutes away. That's Cook Inlet you see over there. It goes out to the Pacific Ocean."

"It's beautiful." I felt a sense of awe unfolding. With my emotions rioting, the beauty reached in and yanked at my heart.

"It is."

We fell quiet for the remainder of the drive. After a while, Alex turned off the highway—a not particularly busy highway, by the way—and a few minutes later, the lights of a town became visible. "This is Willow Brook," he said as he turned onto a street.

It was approaching midnight, so all the shops were closed, but the streetlights were on. The main street showed a cute town with storefronts and signs glowing in the darkness.

"We'll get coffee here in the morning," he said as we passed a place with a sign labeled *Firehouse Café*.

In another few minutes, Alex pulled up to a small house in the darkness. Two lights flanked the front door. "Here we are."

He insisted on taking my bag, and my footsteps crunched on the gravel as I followed him across the driveway and up the stairs onto the small porch. Looking around, I saw nothing but trees although I knew houses were nearby because we had passed them on the way.

I couldn't see much beyond the small pool of illumination cast by the lights on either side of the door. We stepped into a tiled entryway, and Alex flicked on the lights. From there, I could see directly across the open room to a wall of windows that offered a view of the mountains with the moon above them.

"It's so pretty," I said softly.

"It's hard not to have a house with a view in Alaska," he commented with a shrug. "You can hang your coat here."

He was pointing at a coatrack standing by the door. I took off my shoes and hung up my coat, following him as he crossed through the living room and passed an island, which delineated the kitchen, to a door on one side of the main area.

He led me into what I presumed was the master

bedroom. It also had windows offering a view of the moon over the mountains and a giant bed.

Alex wheeled my suitcase through another door on the side of the room. Following him, I realized he had a walk-in closet with shelving on both sides. He lifted my suitcase and set it on top of a dresser. "You can leave this here."

He then took me on a quick tour. There was his bedroom, which had a nice bathroom with a gigantic tub. The living room and kitchen area were decorated in muted colors, along with the rest of the place. There was another bedroom opposite Alex's on the other side of the living room, and a bathroom with a washer and dryer.

When we were back in the living room, I commented, "This is really nice. You decorated it well."

Alex cast me a sheepish grin. "My mother and Holly decorated it. I built it, though. Nate helped me. Are you hungry? I knew you were going to be landing late, so I got some pizza that I could reheat if you were hungry when you got here."

Just as I was about to open my mouth and refuse, my stomach let out a rumble.

Alex chuckled. "I'll heat that pizza up now."

I didn't remember falling asleep on the couch after we ate, but I came awake when Alex lifted me into his arms. "We're going to bed," he murmured as he pressed his lips against my temple.

The tension from a long day of travel unraveled in my body as I fell asleep wrapped in Alex's embrace.

Chapter Twenty-Four

ALEX

Delilah's cheeks were still pink from our shower. I wasn't about to let her shower alone, so we'd showered together before hopping in my truck to go to town for breakfast. Her hair was still damp, and she lifted a hand and patted it lightly. "Are you sure?"

"Am I sure about what?"

"For me to go out like this with wet hair."

I bit back a smile. "Of course. My hair's still wet." I gestured to my damp locks.

She rolled her eyes, letting out a little huff. "You're a guy."

Reaching across the console, I caught her hand and gave it a quick squeeze. "Delilah, this is Alaska. You could show up in rubber boots in one of the nicer restaurants, and it would be okay. We're just getting coffee. I promise it's totally casual."

"Yeah, but who are we going to run into? This is your hometown."

"I didn't plan to meet anyone, so if we do run into anyone, it'll be by chance."

"Oh my God, is this the kind of place your parents go? What if we run into them by chance?"

This time, I couldn't hold back my laughter. "Babe, they really wouldn't care. I've never known you to worry so much about how you looked. What gives?"

As I turned onto Main Street in Willow Brook, I stole a glance at her. She looked a little tense, and my heart gave a funny twist.

"I don't know. It's just, this is your world, and I don't want to make a bad impression."

"You already met Holly. She's probably the toughest customer in my family. You weren't worried when we were at the ski lodge."

I turned into the parking lot at Firehouse Café, aiming for a spot in the back corner.

"Yeah, but that was unexpected. I didn't have time to worry," Delilah explained.

"I won't tell you not to worry because I find whenever people say that to me, it doesn't help at all."

Delilah cast me a big smile. "Thank you. When people tell me not to worry about things, it just makes me feel silly. Then I worry about worrying. It's like I'm doing something wrong."

"Exactly. I'll just say this: you're beautiful, and it's pretty much impossible for you to make a bad impression."

Delilah twisted her mouth sideways, but she didn't protest further. A moment later, I held the door for her, reaching for her hand as I let it close behind us. The bell jingled above. I watched Delilah glance around the space.

Firehouse Café had been around since I was a kid. I took the moment to see it through her eyes. The café was in the town's old fire station. The tall, square garage had been transformed into seating for diners with an open-style bakery and kitchen. The fire poles were painted brightly with fireweed flowers, square wooden tables were scattered about for seating, and local artwork hung on the walls.

A few familiar faces were present, but none of my family or close friends happened to be here. I let out a silent sigh of relief. While I took comfort from and appreciated the embrace of having family and friends close, I sensed Delilah was tense about it. I knew enough about her childhood now to understand.

Delilah had been managing her life independently since she was a child. I wanted her to learn it was okay to lean on someone else. I just had to figure out how to make that magic happen.

"Should we get in line or get a table?" Delilah asked, glancing up at me.

I resisted the urge to kiss her. Delilah didn't wear makeup, and fresh-faced with rosy cheeks in the morning, she was gorgeous. Her pink lips were plump from me kissing her senseless in the shower not too long ago.

I resisted the urge, knowing she would not appreciate too much PDA. "Either," I replied with a shrug. "If we grab a table, someone will come wait on us, but there are no menus. You might want to order at the counter, so you can choose what you want for breakfast from the chalkboard."

Delilah moved toward the counter, and I followed, keeping a hold of her hand. Two women holding hands stepped aside just as we got there.

Janet beamed at us. "Hi, Alex. Who's your friend?" Janet's perceptive gaze bounced down to where my hand clasped Delilah's.

"This is Delilah," I replied. "She's visiting from North Carolina, same town where Remy's from."

I didn't know how it was physically possible, but Janet's smile got even wider when she looked toward Delilah. "So nice to meet you. Welcome to our town. What can I get you two this morning?"

I was relieved Janet kept it brief. She was known for being chatty; however, she was too kind to tease Delilah. I ordered my coffee and a bagel with cream cheese while Delilah scanned the chalkboard menu above.

"I'll take a plain coffee," she said. "The bagel with smoked salmon cream cheese sounds good too."

"Oh, it is," I assured her.

"Just put that on my tab," I said, glancing back at Janet.

"You got it. Go ahead and have a seat."

A few people had already come in behind us, so we got out of the way and grabbed a table in the corner by the windows.

"This place is cute," Delilah offered as she shrugged out of her jacket and hung it over the back of her chair.

"It is. Used to be the town's fire station."

"Janet seems nice," she added.

"She's the best. She's a friend of my mom's, so I should warn you, she'll probably text my mom to let her know she met you first."

Delilah's cheeks went a little pink. She shook her head slightly, her lashes sweeping down as she unrolled the napkin around the silverware on the table by her elbow.

Janet had just brought us our coffee when Remy Martin walked in. His eyes scanned in the room, widening slightly when they landed on Delilah. He crossed over to us immediately. "Hey, girl," he said, stopping by our table.

Delilah looked up, a smile breaking across her face. "Hey, Remy!"

She stood and gave him a quick hug. I was oddly relieved to see her slightly guarded even with someone she'd known for years. Relieved and a little sad. Remy glanced between us. I'd run into him just last week and mentioned Delilah would be here. I wasn't so sure he'd believed me.

"When did you get here?" he asked.

"Late last night. After midnight, actually, so I guess it was this morning," she offered.

"Hi there, Remy." Janet bustled over with our bagels and

cream cheese. "Would you like me to prep your usual?" she asked after she set our plates down in front of us.

"Of course. Thanks, Janet!" he called. She was already hurrying back to the counter where someone else was waiting.

"We should have dinner," Remy said. "I don't have much time to chat now because I'm on my way to the station for a shift. Rachel would love to see you."

Delilah looked toward me, and I nodded. "Tell me what works. We're having dinner with my parents tonight, but any other night is fine with me."

"Are you working this week?" he asked

"I'm just on call for emergencies."

"Got it. Well, I'll check with Rachel, and I'll text you, okay?"

"Sounds good, man."

Remy tapped Delilah lightly on the shoulder as he turned away.

Delilah took a bite of her bagel, letting out a moan. "Oh, my God," she said after she finished chewing. "This is incredible."

I grinned. "Oh, yeah. Don't go thinking that's imported salmon. Probably caught right here in Cook Inlet. Were you close to Remy growing up?" I asked between bites of my own bagel and sips of coffee.

Delilah cocked her head to the side, lifting one hand and swiveling it side to side in the air. "Sort of. Shay and I were in high school together, so obviously, I know her better. He was a few years ahead of us. He's that kind of friend. Like I've known him forever, but we weren't really close." Before I could say anything else, she added, "So we're having dinner with your parents tonight?"

I silently swore. Now, she was probably going to worry about it all day.

"Do you mind? Because we can change plans. I just

figured we might as well because you're here. Holly and Nate will be there."

Delilah's eyes searched my face, but she stayed quiet, finally offering, "That's okay. I figured I would meet them. This way I'll only obsess all day today."

"I swear they don't bite."

She was quiet for a few minutes, and the sound of people talking in the background filled the next few moments as we ate. I thought she was going to drop it, but she blurted out, "I've never met anyone's parents."

Looking across at her, I said the only thing that came to mind. "I've never brought anyone home to meet my parents."

Chapter Twenty-Five

DELILAH

"So, what do you do?" Alex's mother, Leslie, asked.

This was, of course, a perfectly reasonable, polite, and expected question. It's just it didn't feel great to tell his mother I was a bartender.

But I prided myself on being honest. "I bartend. I'm also in nursing school," I added, hoping whatever I did with my face resembled a smile.

I was *way* too tense about meeting Alex's parents.

Leslie smiled. "Oh, I bartended for a few years when I was in college. It's a great way to make money and have a flexible schedule. Holly mentioned you were in nursing school. How's it going?"

"Okay, I guess. I'm doing classes while I work, so it's mostly online. Next spring, I'll need to line up my internship."

His mother nodded again. "I'll be honest, I enjoyed being a nurse, but I did *not* miss school. It was a ton of work. I can't believe you're doing it while you're also working full-time."

I shrugged. "It's the only way to afford it. After my

internship next year, I'll be done."

Just then, Alex and his father returned from the garage where Alex had been looking at something on his father's car. "When's dinner going to be ready?" his father, Russell, asked.

Alex's mother cast me an apologetic smile. "He's always starving. I've never figured out how to manage that, despite over thirty-five years of marriage."

Russell cast me an unabashed grin. "It's just because she's such a good cook."

Leslie stood from where we were seated in a pair of chairs, crossing over to him. He leaned over and dusted a kiss across her lips. "Such a charmer. About fifteen minutes, let me go check the oven," she replied. "Do you know when Holly and Nate will be here?"

Alex had crossed the room to stand beside me where I was sitting in a comfortable chair. He looked at his watch. "She said fifteen minutes ago, but obviously, they're late." He glanced down at me. "Would you like something to drink?"

I started to shake my head, but then Leslie spoke. "Oh, my goodness! I didn't offer you something to drink yet. Alex, fix that now."

I felt his hand come to rest on my shoulder, and that subtle touch somehow eased the anxiety starting to spin in my chest. "They have plenty of options. Wine, beer, water, soda, juice, and I don't know, probably something else," Alex offered with a grin.

"What are you having?"

"I'm going to grab a beer."

"I'll take whatever you're having."

His eyes searched mine briefly. "You don't have to. If you prefer something else, all you have to do is say so."

"I like beer. I promise I'm not having it just because you are," I offered with a smile.

Alex departed the living room, stepping through the archway into a kitchen. A moment later, he returned with two bottles of beer in his hands. He sat down in a chair beside me. His parents' house was comfortable. The ceilings were tall with light coming in through the windows that looked out over a field. There was a big sectional sofa and two comfy chairs angled toward each other with a small table between them.

I wanted to relax. I wasn't normally all that shy. I couldn't be when I worked at a bar all the time. But this first—meeting a man's parents, a man who was coming to mean so very much to me—had me feeling tongue-tied and twisted up inside with nervousness.

Alex caught my eyes. "You don't need to worry. They already love you," he said in a low voice.

I bit my lip before I took a swallow of my beer. "This is a nice place," I offered, not really wanting to dwell on how I was feeling.

"It is."

Glancing out the window, I asked, "Is there anywhere that doesn't have a pretty view in Alaska?"

He chuckled. "Probably not. I could say the same about the mountains in North Carolina."

"True, but everything here is so much bigger."

Alex was nodding when the front door opened, and Holly and Nate entered. Holly crossed the room to me immediately. Setting my beer on the table beside my chair, I stood to greet her and was surprised when Holly pulled me into a big hug.

"Oh, my gosh!" she said when she stepped back. "It's so great that you're here. What do you think of Willow Brook so far?"

"It's beautiful," I began, not able to get anything else out.

Nate was saying something to Alex, and then Alex's parents were back in the room with everyone greeting each other. I felt like an interloper. I didn't have experience with a family like this—one where everyone was nice and clearly held an easy, genuine affection for each other.

My manners got me through it, and it wasn't long before we were sitting at the dinner table. We'd never even had a dining room table in the various homes I shared with my parents growing up. I imagined Holly and Alex probably sat down for dinner with their parents every night when they were kids.

"Let's say grace," his mother said.

Everyone bowed their heads. "Amen," his father finished after rattling off the fastest prayer I'd ever heard.

I had to bite my lip to keep from giggling when Holly caught my eyes from across the table, hers dancing with mirth. "Laugh away. We used to have prayer races when we were growing up."

I laughed. "I don't even know what that means."

"We were always starving, so we would see whoever could say grace the fastest," Alex explained from my side.

Dinner was delicious. His mother had made salmon seasoned with lemon and other spices and a rice pilaf with asparagus on the side. I'd just finished when Holly asked, "Did Alex tell you about the option to do your internship at the hospital here in Willow Brook? You should do it. It would be awesome to have you here."

When I looked across the table, she looked so friendly and helpful, I wanted to tell her I'd plan on it. But that was crazy. I didn't live here, and I felt like Alex and I weren't even real. I'd wake up one day, alone in my apartment and remember it was all just a dream.

"He mentioned it," I hedged, pausing to sip my water and carefully put my silverware on my plate.

"Most of those online programs let people do internships all over the place. The hospital here is accredited with all the major nursing associations that approve the programs. If you're worried I would be your boss, I wouldn't. While I am one of the ER supervisors, one of our admin nurses handles the intern supervision. You'd be able to work with me, and it's a fun group. I hope you'll seriously think about it."

Chapter Twenty-Six

ALEX

Delilah was nervous. Dinner with my family had gone as well as it could, or so I thought. Except for the fact Delilah had been tense the whole time.

Now, it was a few days later, and we were on the way to have dinner with Remy and Rachel. She seemed nervous again. We were meeting at Wildlands because Delilah said she wanted to see the place since I mentioned it was where I most often went out to meet friends.

I cut the engine on my truck. As quiet surrounded us in my truck cab, the call of an eagle screeched outside.

"What's that?" She glanced toward me.

"An eagle. They often perch in the trees along the lake."

We got out, and I beckoned for her to follow me to the edge of the parking lot behind Wildlands. The lake spread out before us, glimmering with streaks of tangerine, red, and gold reflected from the sky as the sun began to set.

"It's so beautiful here," Delilah breathed at my side.

"It is." Reaching over, I caught her hand, my heart giving a little kick when she easily laced her fingers into mine.

I wanted her to stop worrying, but then I didn't know

how to make sense of any of this either. Because no matter how I sliced it, one of us would have to make a big change for us to be together. I shied away from thinking about that because I wasn't ready to decide. I wanted it to be easier, and that made me feel like a coward.

When another eagle called, I scanned the shoreline, my eyes finally landing on an eagle perched in a spruce tree. "Hang on." I released her hand and jogged the short distance back to my truck. Returning a moment later, I handed her a small pair of binoculars I kept in my glove compartment. The eagle called again, and I pointed in its direction to one side.

Delilah lifted the binoculars, scanning until she stilled. "Oh, wow. I've never actually seen one in the wild."

"If you want to see a lot of eagles, I'll take you to the town's transfer station," I commented.

Delilah watched as the eagle took flight, its silhouette dark against the backdrop of the dusky sky. After it disappeared from sight, she lowered the binoculars and looked toward me. "The transfer station? Not exactly romantic, Alex," she teased.

I chuckled as she handed the binoculars back to me. "I didn't say it was romantic, but you're guaranteed to see a lot of eagles there. Come on." I reached for her hand again. "Remy and Rachel are probably already here. Have you met Rachel before?"

We paused by the truck, and I returned the binoculars to the glove compartment. When we were walking again, Delilah replied, "Just once. Remy brought her to the bar one time when they were visiting."

More and more, I was getting a sense of just how thoroughly Delilah guarded herself. She didn't spend much time with someone she even considered a friend. I supposed I should feel lucky she was letting me in at all.

A few minutes later, Remy was asking, "How long are you here?"

"Just in town through the end of this week. I have to be back in Stolen Hearts Valley for work and school," Delilah replied.

"You could do school anywhere," I commented, surprising myself.

I felt Delilah's sharp gaze on mine for a moment, but I didn't look away. For some reason, I wanted to push her a little bit. More and more, I was beginning to understand that I was going to have to pull off a freaking magic trick to win her trust. I couldn't go too fast, but if I never pushed, she'd never let me in.

When she finally looked away, Rachel commented, "So true. I hear from Holly she's trying to persuade you to do your internship at the hospital here. It's a good place. You could also do it where I work."

Delilah looked puzzled, but a waitress paused by our table. While Remy started ordering, Rachel clarified, "I'm a medical assistant. I work at a family practice office here in Willow Brook. We have two doctors, one full-time and one part-time, but we also have nurses on staff. If you did it there, my boss, Charlie, would be your supervisor. She's awesome."

Remy interjected, "I ordered us a pitcher of beer and a couple of appetizers. I hope that's okay." He rested his arm over Rachel's shoulders, the comfort between them evident. "What's this about Charlie?" he asked.

"I was telling Delilah she could consider doing her internship at my office. Charlie's a great boss," Rachel explained.

"She's not my boss," Remy said with a slow smile. "But she's great."

"I'm not sure what I'm going to do," Delilah said. "I mean, I live in North Carolina right now."

Remy grinned and waggled his eyebrows. "You should move here. I did, and I fucking love it. I miss Shay and my friends there, but Willow Brook is a great place to live."

I made a mental note to thank Remy the next time I saw him. Delilah was noncommittal, and simply said, "I'll just have to see where things are at next fall. That's when I finish my last semester before it's time for me to do my internship in the spring."

Our beer and food arrived. Remy asked Delilah about Stolen Hearts Valley. Rachel was my personal cheerleader for Willow Brook throughout dinner.

At one point, Remy asked, "How are your parents?"

Delilah's lips pressed into a line. "They're okay," she replied, offering no additional information.

I didn't know why, but sadness sliced through me at that. Not with Delilah specifically but with how much her default was to keep everything shut down and protected. Her father was dying, and she wasn't even talking about it.

We left a little while later, and on the drive home, I couldn't help asking, "Tell me something, do you have any close friends?"

I could feel her eyes practically burning into me. "Yes. Why do you ask?"

"Because even with the people you call friends, you don't talk about your dad being sick."

I could practically feel a flash of fire in the air. "I depend on myself, and that's it. I'm the only person I've ever been able to depend on," she said stiffly.

When I glanced to the side, she had crossed her arms and was staring out the window. "Delilah, I didn't mean—"

She glanced over, meeting my eyes briefly. "Don't judge my life. I'm not complaining about my life, so don't go thinking that. I didn't have the kind of family you did, so it's different for me."

"Delilah, I'm not judging you. I just wish you'd let yourself count on someone."

"I count on myself."

I was fuming inside, flushed with defensiveness and anger. Obviously, Alex thought everyone should have the kind of life he did with tons of close friends and everybody knowing everything about him.

I swallowed my anger and stayed quiet, watching the mountains as we drove. I loved his parents and his sister, and I loved this cute little town. I could see why Remy fell in love with it when he got a job out here. The word beautiful didn't do it justice. It was breathtaking and stunning, and everybody was freaking nice. Maybe it was because I was with Alex, and it was clear his family was beloved in this town.

People here were genuinely down to earth. That said, if one more person suggested I consider doing my internship here, I was going to scream.

I didn't know why I felt tethered to Stolen Hearts Valley. It wasn't as if I had the kind of network of support Alex did here. I knew I could make any decision right now. I *could* decide to move to Willow Brook, but that meant handing my heart to Alex. And I still wasn't sure if he felt this thing between us to his bones the way I did.

When we got back to his place and walked inside, I still felt unsettled. Following Alex's lead, I hung my jacket on the coatrack by the door. Alex had started to walk through the living room, but he turned and abruptly stopped beside the back of the sofa.

His eyes searched mine. "I didn't mean to upset you."

I opened my mouth to lie and tell him he didn't upset me, but that was not what came out. "I know you didn't mean to. I'm just used to taking care of myself. That's all."

I wondered if my sullen mood had ruined the night, but it didn't matter. The one thing that was magic with Alex and me was our chemistry that just wouldn't quit. There was a lamp on in the corner. As I held his dark eyes, my pulse began to thrum, and the unsettled feeling spun into the heat instantly dancing through my veins.

If one thing was guaranteed to make me forget, it was losing myself in him and letting the flames eclipse all thought. Crossing to him, I placed my palm flat on his chest. I felt his heart leap in reaction.

"Do we have to talk?" I asked, letting my hands slide over his chest and down across his muscled abs to cup his cock through his jeans, which was already swollen under my touch.

"Delilah," he began, almost as if he was going to try to keep on talking about this.

"That wasn't really a question, Alex," I murmured as I leaned up and pressed an open-mouthed kiss on the side of his neck.

Alex's eyes darkened further, and I heard the sharp intake of his breath when I stroked boldly over his arousal.

"What are you doing?" he rasped, his voice low and taut.

"I'm definitely not in the mood to keep talking. We only have two more nights before I have to go back home."

Although desire was driving me, a fierce, emotional need lay claim to me again and again and again with Alex. My heart gave a sharp twist in my chest when I voiced the obvious. Yet again, my time with Alex was only temporary, just a mirage.

I felt almost frantic. I didn't want to contemplate the fact I was leaving. I stroked up and down his hard length again. On the heels of a ragged breath, his hand was lacing in my hair, and his mouth was on mine. In a burning hot second, our kiss was devouring—a messy tangle of lips and tongue.

With need driving me, I tore at the buttons of his fly, letting out a loud moan in his mouth when I slid my hand into his boxers and curled my palm around his velvety arousal.

Alex tore his lips from mine and lifted his head. "Fuck, Delilah."

With the couch right behind him, I gave him a little push, and his hips bumped into it. When I stroked again, he muttered something unintelligible before his hips settled on the back edge of the couch.

I shoved his jeans and boxers down a little to gain access. Letting my eyes fall, I slid my thumb over the drop of pre-cum rolling out of the tip. Leaning down, I swirled my tongue around the thick crown.

I heard him groan, murmuring, "Sweetheart."

Opening my lips, I sucked on his cock, sliding down slowly as I took him into my mouth fully. The salty tang of him danced across my tongue as I settled in. Gripping the base, I teased my tongue along the underside, creating suction with every stroke.

Alex muttered something roughly. His hand tangled in my hair, and I savored the sharp sting on my scalp. I felt his cock swell, and then he was gasping my name. I lifted my head as I dragged my tongue up once more.

"Delilah." His eyes were wild and dark on mine.

"Mm-hmm?" Another tease of my tongue around the thick crown of his cock.

"I want to be inside you," he said bluntly.

He could be a little bossy, and I didn't mind it, not one bit. My libido thought it was the best thing ever. I didn't even think. I slowly straightened, and before I knew it, he had me bent over the couch with my hands digging into the cushions.

I savored the sting of his palm on my bottom when he lightly slapped it. His fingers teased between my legs. I was drenched, the juices of my arousal slick on my thighs.

"You like that," he murmured when he nipped my earlobe.

Biting my lip, I tried to hold in my whimper, but I couldn't. Alex took the best care of me when it came to this. I felt empty, desperate for him to fill me, to assuage the need sizzling through my body.

His palm slid over my bottom, squeezing me, and I felt the tease of his fingers along my swollen pussy. "Alex," I begged.

"Tell me what you need."

Chapter Twenty-Eight

ALEX

"You, I need you," Delilah gasped.

I couldn't tease her any longer. I was already too close to the end of my tether. Ever since she'd nearly pushed me over the edge with her naughty mouth, I'd been clinging to my control.

I gripped my cock in my fist, looking down at her pink, glistening pussy. With her bent over, and her lush bottom tipped up, need sizzled at the base of my spine, my balls already tightening in anticipation. Reaching into my back pocket, I snagged the condom I'd tucked in my wallet earlier tonight—because I'd learned I needed to be prepared at all times when I was with her.

I smoothed it on and dragged my cockhead through her juices. She arched her back more deeply, raising her bottom. "Alex." Her voice was frayed, ragged with desire.

I filled her in one deep stroke, gripping her hip with my hand as she let out a low cry. I forced myself to hold still for a minute, gritting my teeth as her channel rippled around my cock. She didn't let me stay still for long, not when she pushed back against me.

Drawing back, I stroked into her snug core, my ferocious need for her sizzling through me. She was already at the edge. I could feel it as she clamped around me. Curling over her, I reached around and teased my fingers over her swollen clit.

She came in a noisy rush, gasping my name between broken cries. I could barely hear her when my own release crashed over me.

My breath came in heaves as the intensity subsided, like the tide slowly rolling out. After a minute, I pulled myself together and lifted her into my arms.

––––––––

Waking up with Delilah was something I could get used to. The last morning before the day she was supposed to leave, I woke before her. The days were already getting noticeably longer here in Alaska. Sunshine fell through the windows in my bedroom in a bright, golden spring light.

Propping myself up on an elbow, I looked down at Delilah. Her dark hair was tangled on the pillow. She was curled on her side with her bottom nestled against my arousal. I was forever waking up with a hard-on with her. My body knew what it wanted.

I loved seeing her asleep because the lines of tension smoothed away from her face, and she looked so unguarded. Her cheeks were a little flushed, and her hands were curled up under her chin. My heart gave a wobbly thump in my chest. I didn't want tomorrow to come. I didn't want her to leave.

We had lunch at Firehouse Café. "It's my favorite place in Willow Brook," Delilah had said.

She'd arrived only six days ago, yet today, I was realizing just how comfortable I'd become with her presence. On the one hand, it felt as if she'd been here much longer. On the other, it felt as if we'd only had a fraction of the time I wanted with her. My internal calculation of time didn't matter, not one iota, because she was leaving tomorrow.

Janet stopped by our table to pick up our plates. Her cheeks plumped with her smile as she looked back and forth between us with her brown eyes twinkling. "Now, Delilah, I hear you're trying to decide between your internship at the emergency department or at the family clinic. What are you thinking?"

Delilah looked startled. Her eyes widened, her mouth parting before she closed it quickly. "I definitely don't know," she finally said.

An uneasy feeling slithered up my spine. I knew she didn't know, but I *wanted* her to know.

A few minutes later, we climbed in my truck. Delilah was quiet as I started it up and turned out of the parking lot in the direction of my parents' place, which was on the way home.

Out of nowhere, or so it felt, Delilah asked, "Are you telling people I'm coming back for my internship?"

Fuck. I did not need Delilah getting more squirrelly than she already was about this.

"I haven't said anything to anyone. I'm guessing you should ask Holly or Rachel about that. Holly is the likely culprit."

Delilah was quiet long enough that I stole a glance at her. She was looking out the window, those familiar lines of tension around her mouth with her shoulders held stiffly.

"Are you even thinking about it?" I heard myself asking.

I didn't see it because I looked ahead again, but I felt Delilah's head whip in my direction. "I don't know. Obviously with people asking about it, I'm thinking about it. But what are we doing? Alex. It seems crazy to me to move across the country. The only reason I would come here would be because of you."

I looked her way, practically feeling the burn of her gaze. "I would move across the country for you."

Chapter Twenty-Nine

DELILAH

May

I would move across the country for you.

That one sentence from Alex had been spinning a circle in my thoughts for weeks. I felt a little crazy.

I took one last look at my father, who was sound asleep and had been for the entirety of my visit this afternoon, before standing and leaving the room quietly. My mother was in the kitchen planting seedlings in her flower boxes. She would put them out to hang on her deck railings soon.

She looked up, her eyes meeting mine as I crossed into the kitchen. "He still sleeping?"

I nodded. "Oh, yeah. When he's awake, how is he doing?"

My mother looked down as she carefully used her fingertips to pat the soil. "He's only awake for an hour here and there. I think he mostly feels tired. They're giving him enough pain medication that I don't think he's in a lot of pain, so for that, I'm grateful." She looked up at me again as she dusted the potting soil off her fingertips. "How are you?"

"I'm okay. Do we have any updates from his doctor or the hospice program?"

"Nothing new. They don't expect him to make it for more than a few months. That hasn't changed."

"Isn't that what they said when he was first diagnosed?"

My mother stood and crossed to the sink where she rinsed her hands as she replied, "That is what they said. The nurses tell me they've seen cases with someone this far along where they dwindle a while before finally passing." My mother turned and dried her hands on a dish towel before hanging it over the oven handle.

I took a deep breath, letting it out slowly. "Okay. I just wish we knew more."

My mother cocked her head to the side. "Do you want to know exactly when he's going to pass? Hon, life very rarely gives us guarantees like that. We are all guaranteed to die, but precisely when is hard to know. Even with someone as sick as your father."

"I know, I know," I replied, idly rubbing my knuckles over my breastbone. There was a burning sensation in my throat and heart.

"Ever since you were a little girl, you always wanted to have guarantees. Every time we moved, you would say, 'Tell me how long we're going to stay here. Exactly.'" Her mouth twisted in a sad smile. "Of course, I understand now that the uncertainty you experienced when you were growing up is precisely why you look for certainty now. I didn't understand it so much then."

That burning sensation intensified. I turned and quickly walked to look out the windows as I crossed my arms over my chest. "Maybe so," I said, striving to keep my tone casual and noncommittal.

"How was your trip to Alaska? You haven't said anything since you got back." My mother's voice became louder as she crossed the room to stand beside me.

I scanned the view of Stolen Hearts Valley and my grandmother's yard. Spring was here. I could see the green shoots from the bulbs coming up in the flower beds, and the daffodils had already bloomed under one of the trees. Everything was becoming lush and green. My mother was already busy with the greenhouse and landscaping business.

"Delilah?" my mother prompted. "Hon, are you okay?"

Sliding my eyes sideways, I shrugged. "I guess. Dad and I were never close, but I'm sad he's dying."

It should've given me pause that I preferred to talk about my father's death than answer my mother's polite question about my trip to Alaska. It's just her observation about my desire for guarantees in life bumped up against everything I was struggling with around Alex and me.

My mother wrapped her arm around my shoulders and gave me a gentle squeeze. "I know, hon."

I felt my phone vibrate in my pocket, the sound snapping me into the moment. Sliding it out, I looked down to see my calendar reminder that I had a shift at the bar tonight. "I gotta go, Mom."

Her arm slid off my shoulders, and she walked me out to my car. I rolled the window down after I started it. "If Dad takes a turn, you'll call me, right?"

"Of course. Maybe next time you come over, you can tell me how your trip to Alaska was."

———

Three weeks later

"Here you go," I said quickly as I slid a beer bottle over the bar with one hand.

I was spinning away and already taking another order

before I heard, "Thank you, gorgeous. Can I get your number?"

"Absolutely not," I called in return, flipping the guy my middle finger.

Fortunately, I worked in a bar where the management was entirely supportive of us being as blunt as necessary with rude, pushy, and inappropriate customers. Navigating the frequent comments thrown my way was simply a part of being a bartender and a woman. For the most part, I didn't even blink. Tonight, I was snappier than usual, my patience on edge. Perhaps because last week I'd told Alex we should stop trying to carry on the charade that we would someday be able to take things to the next level. I'd broken my own damn heart.

He tried to argue, and he kept calling me. I'd finally silenced his number because it hurt to see the record of calls I was ignoring. Silencing, that handy feature of modern technology. It wasn't quite as harsh as blocking, but it allowed me to ignore him for the time being.

I'd been heartsick ever since. I didn't like to think of myself as someone who played games, but I couldn't help but wonder if a subconscious part of me *was* playing games. Because it hurt me that he hadn't tried harder to argue the point. His calls had tapered off, and I hated it, which was ridiculous. I felt ashamed for even thinking that.

I kept serving drinks and got through the night. Gobs of tips were pouring in tonight. There was a wedding at the winery, which meant we got a ton of overflow business and people with cash to spend. After closing, I was wiping down the bar when Jade Cole commented, "Girl, you are cranky. What gives? And I say that with all love because you know my general default is cranky."

I dipped a towel into the bleach mixture and kept wiping down the bar in swift, efficient motions. Jade was a friend and filled in at the bar whenever we needed extra help.

Looking up, I met her eyes. "My schedule is nuts. I'm too

busy to stay sane between work and school." Okay, so that *was* true. Yet I was also avoiding the truth behind my mood.

Jade was quiet for a beat before asking, "How are things with Alex?"

The minute I looked up really fast, I knew I had given myself away. Jade's eyes took on a gleam. "I met him that one night when y'all stopped by the bar. Don't forget I also covered for you when you went to Alaska."

I finished wiping down the bar and tossed the towel into the laundry bin we kept right behind the bar during the cleanup phase every night. Sliding my hips on the back of a barstool, I leaned my face in my hands. My sigh filtered through my fingers.

I refused to be a coward, so I lifted my head and met her gaze. "I broke things off with him. It made no sense. Not with him there and me here. You know?"

Jade gave me a long considering look as she rinsed her hands under the faucet in the sink on the other side of the bar. "I don't know. Alex seems like a good guy. You don't talk much about your family, but is that what's holding you here? Because why not go to Alaska?"

Chapter Thirty

ALEX

I almost threw my phone against the wall. Rex Masters looked at me from across his desk at the police station in Willow Brook. "Woman troubles?" he asked with a wry grin.

I leaned back in the chair where I sat in his office and ran a hand through my hair. "Why is she fucking not answering my calls?" I asked.

Rex gave me a sympathetic look, and I hated it. "Obviously, I can't answer that. I can only tell you she didn't actually block your number." I'd stopped by the police station to ask Rex if there was any way to tell if a number was blocked. He'd done me a favor and checked, only to learn Delilah hadn't blocked me. That just meant she was doing a fantastic job of ignoring every call and text from me.

"I know, Rex."

At that moment, there was a knock on his door. Rex called, "Come in!"

Rex's son and a friend of mine, Cade Masters, stepped into the room. Rex was the police chief here in Willow Brook while Cade was the superintendent for one of the hotshot fire crews stationed in Willow Brook.

"Oh," Cade said, his brows hitching up when he saw me. "Sorry to interrupt."

"Hey, it's no problem," I said as I stood from my chair.

"Alex is having woman problems," Rex offered. *Unnecessarily*, I thought.

Cade divided a look between us and stayed quiet, although his lips twitched slightly. He looked back toward his father. "Just checking to see if you want me to drop you off to pick up your car from the mechanic this afternoon."

"I'd love a ride over there," Rex said. "When are you leaving?"

Cade glanced at his watch. "In about five minutes. Will that work?"

"I'll make it work." As I turned to leave, Rex called, "Alex?"

"Yeah?" I turned at the doorway to look back at him.

"Fight for her if she means that much to you."

"I'll try."

Cade followed me down the hall. He remained quiet until we stepped out into the parking lot. "I'm trying to figure out why the hell my father's giving you relationship advice."

I met his eyes and rolled mine. "I'm just being an idiot. I came to ask him if he could verify if my number was blocked. It's not."

Cade started to reply when a truck turned into the parking lot, emblazoned with the label Kick A** Construction. He cracked a wide smile as his wife, Amelia, parked and climbed out quickly. She angled straight for us where we stood beside the doors to the station. Amelia was tall and leggy, and totally in love with her husband. Cade demonstrated just how whipped he still was by her when he jogged a few steps to close the distance between them and pull her in for a kiss.

Amelia's cheeks were pink when she drew away with a laugh a moment later. "I was just coming to see if you wanted me to take you over to pick up your dad's truck," she said, glancing in my direction with a quick smile.

"Funny you mention that," I called over. "Guess you guys are gonna have to arm wrestle for who takes Rex over to get it. I'd offer to help, but I don't think it's necessary at this point."

Amelia chuckled. "What are you doing here?"

"Asking my dad for relationship advice," Cade said, his tone dry.

Amelia looked genuinely baffled.

"Ignore him," I said.

"Is Delilah coming back?" Amelia asked.

Before I could even answer, Beck Steele came out the back door of the station. Great, just fucking great. Beck never missed a chance to tease anyone. As soon as he saw us, he walked right over. "What's up?"

Amelia looked toward Beck. "Apparently, Alex is here asking Rex for relationship advice."

Beck's eyes widened comically as he looked from Amelia to me. "Huh?"

"Fuck my life," I muttered. "That's not exactly what happened."

"You didn't answer my question, though. Is Delilah coming back?" Amelia repeated.

"I don't know," I said with a sigh. "I would like to say she would, but I don't think so. She's not making it easy. She won't talk to me right now."

Beck hooked his thumb in the pocket of his jeans and gave me a long look. "Dude, if you need relationship advice about women who don't make it easy, I'm your go-to guy. Maisie loves me," he said, referencing his wife, Maisie, who did, in fact, appear to love him deeply. Maisie definitely hadn't made it easy on Beck when they first got together.

"Yeah, well, Maisie's here in Willow Brook. Delilah's in North Carolina. It's a whole lot harder with thousands of miles in the way." I was feeling irritated.

Beck looked at me quietly, and I shifted my shoulders uneasily. As much as Beck loved to joke around, he was disarmingly perceptive sometimes. "Dude, if she means that much, then I'd say get your ass to North Carolina."

———

I contemplated my options for how the hell to get a hold of Delilah. Because even though she was ignoring me, I sensed she was doing it more out of self-preservation than anything else.

At my wits' end, I called Remy. He answered on the second ring. "What's up?"

"Hey, Remy, it's Alex. I need a favor."

"Happy to help. What do you need?"

"Is there any way you can get a message to Delilah for me?"

A few days later, after Remy assured me he would reach out to friends in Stolen Hearts Valley and find a way to get a message to Delilah, I was out at the airport working on a plane engine.

Something weird was going on with this one, and I was carefully taking things apart. As I lifted off the cover where the battery was, there was a loud boom. I pushed out of the compartment quickly, turning to see a small plane that had just landed. Its engine was on fire.

I heard screaming as I started running across the parking lot toward the runway. I could hear other footsteps in the distance. When I got to the plane, I saw the pilot slumped over the steering wheel. Fred was an old friend and had been flying all over Alaska for as long as I could recall. He was unconscious. There were two passengers in the back, already clambering out. I called for them to get out as fast as they could as I yanked the door open to where Fred was. The last thing I remembered was another loud boom just as his weight came into my arms.

Chapter Thirty-One

ALEX

3 a.m. Alaska

As I tried opening my eyes, my thoughts were fuzzy. I stared up at a blank white ceiling. Turning my head sideways, I saw a light blue curtain beside my bed. Just moving my head hurt like hell.

"What the fuck?" I muttered to myself.

Taking in my surroundings, I deduced I was in a hospital bed, and my head throbbed. When I moved to sit up, I discovered I was too weak and collapsed against the pillows.

I tried to remember what happened. It took a moment, but I recalled the engine exploding on Fred's plane when he landed and running over to check. The last thing I recalled was pulling him out while the passengers leaped to the ground. My memory was a giant blank spot after that.

Yet again, I tried to sit up. When I struggled to breathe, I fell into the pillows again. "Fuck."

Looking around, I couldn't tell if I was alone or not. There was a window to the side of my bed, and it was barely light out. I could tell I was in Willow Brook because I could see the lights from downtown just outside the hospital. I looked around my bed, noticing that I had an IV in one arm.

My eyes finally landed on what I presumed was the call button for the nurses. I pressed the button for help.

In another moment, I heard the door opening and footsteps following before the curtain was pushed back. "Well, hello there, how are you, Alex?" the nurse asked.

"What the hell is going on?" I recognized the nurse right away. Chris Grant was one of Holly's good friends at the hospital here. "How did I luck into getting you?"

Chris smiled. "We have somebody on vacation this week, so I'm covering a few night shifts. Do you remember what happened?" He stepped to the monitor beside my bed to check a few things.

"The last thing I remember is pulling Fred out of the plane. The passengers were jumping out and seemed okay. I can't remember anything else. Can you fill me in? For starters, can you tell me if Fred is okay?"

Chris pulled a chair over and sat down beside my bed. "Sure thing. Fred is fine. He's asleep in the bed beside you. You both got knocked out when one of the plane engines exploded. Fortunately, the passengers were fine. They dragged you both away quickly. I'm guessing you might have some hearing loss, but a specialist will test it later."

I thought I could hear okay, but one of my ears was ringing a little.

"Why am I still here?"

Chris's brows hitched up. "You with all the questions. You just woke up now. You have a minor concussion. You were totally out of it. Looks like Fred has a case of blast lung from the explosion. If you do, it's minor because your breathing is much better. We had you on oxygen for a bit, but then your breathing improved. You have some abrasions on your back from being thrown on the pavement from the blast. You're probably gonna be sore as hell, but otherwise, you're okay. You saved Fred's life. If he'd been trapped in the front of the plane when the second explosion happened, it would've been much worse. The front end of the plane caught on fire almost immediately because fuel was already leaking from the first explosion."

I stared at Chris, trying to absorb what happened. "Damn. I can't believe I don't remember that."

"Well, you were knocked unconscious. You can't remember anything when you're unconscious," he said matter-of-factly.

I rolled my eyes. "No wonder it's hard to sit up. My back is sore, and I run out of breath in about a second."

Chris stood from the chair, immediately reaching for something on the wheeled stand by my bed. He put a clip over my thumb. "I want to check your oxygen levels. We might need to give you some more."

After a minute, he shook his head. "No, your level is good. I think you're feeling the strain from the blast."

"Is Fred still on oxygen?"

"Yes, but he'll be okay. He's older, and he was knocked unconscious when the plane landed. He has some bruising to his ribs from the rough landing. He's dozing on pain meds."

"I didn't get any pain meds?" I teased.

Chris angled his head to the side. "Much lower dose. You're younger. You can handle it. If you're in pain, though, just let me know."

I took a breath, silently scanning my body. "I'm sore, but I can deal. Has my family been here?"

Chris sighed. "Are you kidding me? Of course! Holly wanted to treat you herself when the ambulance brought you in with Fred. I had to physically pull her away. Everybody's dozing or guzzling coffee in the waiting room now."

"Who is everybody?"

"Your mom and dad, Holly and Nate. Want to see them?"

"I'd like to. Will it wake Fred up?"

"Let's wheel you out," Chris said in a conspiratorial tone.

With a little help from him, he got me into a wheelchair with my IV to follow along and wheeled me down the hallways. The only sounds at this hour were the hum and beep of hospital machines.

When my wheelchair was turned into the waiting room, emotion tightened in my chest. Holly was asleep, curled up with her knees pulled to her chest and her head resting on Nate's shoulder. He was actually awake. His eyes lifted from the magazine on his lap, and a smile stretched across his face immediately.

Both of my parents were asleep, and I held my finger to my lips. Nate gently shook Holly's shoulder. She came awake instantly, looking up at him before she looked wildly around the room, and her eyes landed on me.

"Alex!" She jumped up as Nate followed her across the room.

"Keep it to a dull roar. I don't want to wake Mom and Dad up," I said quietly when she reached me.

"Wake them up," she said. "They just want to see you. Then they'll go home and go to sleep."

Holly's voice carried across the room, and my mother lifted her head. In another moment, all of them were surrounding my wheelchair.

"How do you feel?" Holly demanded. "Has Chris checked all of your levels?"

He was standing behind my chair, and I imagined she got an eye roll for that one. "Of course. Everything looks good. He's feeling a little weak, but he's fine."

"How are his oxygen levels?" Holly pressed.

"Within normal limits," Chris replied patiently.

My mom knelt beside my wheelchair, curling her hands around one of mine. "How are you? You gave us a scare."

"I'm fine. A little sore, but I think I'll be all right. I guess they're going to test my hearing later this morning."

"How is it now?" Holly asked, leaning down and looking

at me, her eyes searching my face as if she could somehow suss it out herself now.

"You're plenty loud, so I can hear you fine. I'm not sure. My head still feels a little fuzzy."

Holly straightened, wrapping her arms tightly around her waist. When I looked up at my dad, I met his eyes to see a stoic worry held there. "I'm okay, Dad."

He patted me on the shoulder. "I know. You gave us a scare."

"Fred's okay too. Apparently, he got more pain meds than me," I teased, trying to lighten the moment.

"Of course he does," Holly said. "He's old. He needs to be comfortable."

"You don't want me to be comfortable?" I countered as I looked back at Holly.

"I do, but just comfortable enough."

A tear rolled down her cheek, and she knuckled it away. Nate curled an arm around her shoulders. "It's okay. He's okay."

"I know," Holly sniffed. "But it scared me."

My mother gave my hand another squeeze before straightening and pressing a kiss on my temple.

"Why don't you guys head home and sleep in a bed? I don't even know what time it is," I said, looking around the room before my eyes landed on the clock mounted in the center of the wall. "Damn, it's three in the morning. Go home."

Nate chuckled. "Now that we've all seen you, we'll go home."

"I'm on duty at noon, so I'm going to check on you then," Holly said. "You better be awake."

Chris laughed from over my shoulder. "If he's asleep, let him rest."

After my family left and Chris wheeled me back to my room, he helped me get back in bed. I hated that I needed the help, but I was tired and fucking sore as all hell.

I lay in bed, wondering how to get a hold of Delilah. Just before Chris left the room, I called, "Do you happen to know where my phone is?"

"No clue. I'll check your things. If you had it on you, it's probably in a bag with your clothes. If not, I'll text Holly. She'll chase it down."

Chapter Thirty-Two

DELILAH

Late afternoon North Carolina – the following day

I missed Alex. So much.

I found myself absentmindedly rubbing my knuckles over my heart as if I could somehow assuage the ache there. The ache that was entirely my fault. I was the one who wasn't answering his calls, although he'd all but stopped. At this point, it was my pride keeping me from calling him. Pride and fear I wouldn't find a slew of texts from him when I stopped silencing his notifications. I cheated and checked almost every day anyway.

I arrived early for a shift at the bar. Things were quiet here in the midafternoon. We served lunch, but there was always a lull in the afternoon until around dinnertime. Today, there were a few customers drinking beers and playing cards, and some young kids from a nearby college were playing pool. They were even being quiet. I would take all small miracles.

Griffin looked up as I walked into the back side of the

bar from the hallway. "Hey there. Didn't expect to see you here today. Did Shay get ahold of you?"

His question confused me. "Aren't I on the schedule?" I asked, focusing on the immediate issue.

I quickly crossed over and tapped on the screen of the tablet we had mounted behind the bar that also served as a register. Scrolling through the window for the schedule, I said, "See, I'm right there."

"I know that. I already called Jade and asked her if she could cover. Shay was here looking for you. Your boyfriend got into an accident."

I was getting more confused, my brain not quite catching up to what Griffin was talking about. Although my brain wasn't processing well, my body seemed to know better. Uneasiness tightened in my chest, and dread balled cold in my belly. "What are you talking about?"

"Alex. He was in an accident. I guess Remy called Shay because he didn't have your number, and Shay came here looking for you. I figured you'd want the night off. Jade will be here soon, so don't worry about it."

It felt like static filled my brain, and I distantly heard myself asking numbly, "What happened? He's not my boyfriend. Where is Shay now?" My questions were flying out, and panic was churning inside. I felt lightheaded, and my throat was so tight with my heart racing that I couldn't get a breath.

Griffin's voice broke through the static. "Hey, easy there, Delilah. Sit down." I felt a chair pressing against the backs of my knees, and my hips collapsed with a thump. "I'm calling Shay right now."

In another minute, Griffin actually had a small paper bag in front of me. I stared at him blankly, not understanding what he was doing.

"You're hyperventilating. I need you to hold this over your mouth and take several deep breaths," Griffin said firmly and calmly.

When I didn't move, he held the bag in front of my mouth for me, and I finally curled my hand around it. A few minutes later, I managed to get enough air in my lungs that the lightheaded and dizzy feeling began to recede.

"Shay is on her way back. I caught her before she got on the highway. She's coming to pick you up," Griffin explained when I lowered the bag to my lap.

"Is Alex okay?"

Griffin nodded as I stared at him. He was a handsome guy, but there was no spark, which was convenient because he was a good friend, and I didn't want to ruin it.

"Shay says he's going to be okay. Something to do with an explosion. I'm sorry I don't have more details."

I reached in my pocket for my phone, coming up empty. "Can you go get my purse?"

Without a word, Griffin turned away, pushing through the door into the back hallway. A moment later, he returned and handed me my phone. "I took the liberty of taking it out of your purse. Hope that's okay."

I mumbled my thanks as I pulled up the screen. I saw the missed calls from Shay and then turned on the notifications for Alex's number. I watched silently as a row of texts populated.

"Did you freaking block his number?" Griffin asked.

When I looked up, I didn't realize I was crying until he turned and snagged a cocktail napkin off the stack on the bar. "I'll take that as a yes," he said.

I blew my nose and wiped tears away from my eyes with the balled up napkin. "I didn't block him, but I silenced the notifications from his number. I'm an idiot."

"Tell me something I don't know," Griffin said dryly. "Actually, you're not an idiot, Delilah. You're fucking smart as hell. But you're not really all about hope and love and shit like that."

Just then, I heard Shay's voice as she came through the

door in the front. "There you are! Come on," she said, gesturing for me to follow her.

Standing from the chair, I barely registered Griffin going back into the hallway again. "Where are we going?" I asked because I honestly didn't know.

"To the airport," Shay said as if I should've known this.

Griffin reappeared, handing me my purse and jacket. "Go."

"I'm going to the airport?"

Shay nodded firmly. "That's right. Holly got you the ticket. She thinks Alex will want to see you when he wakes up."

Chapter Thirty-Three

DELILAH

I had to give it to Shay; she was navigating the narrow mountain road that led out of Stolen Hearts Valley to the highway like a champ, smoothly keeping the vehicle on track despite the fast-moving pace. I hadn't thought very much about it and had simply followed her into the truck. I'd learned in the last hour that Shay could be pretty bossy. She insisted we go by my house to get some things. She also told me it was silly for me to bring my car unless I wanted to pay for parking at the airport. I didn't, so I took her suggestion.

I had nothing more than a single backpack with clothes and toiletries stuffed hastily in it.

"How in the world did you end up talking to Holly?" I finally asked.

"Because Remy called me. He told me he was giving her my number. I've met her before when we've been out to visit Remy and Rachel. Holly got you a ticket and told me it was already waiting for you at the counter. She sent the email confirmation to me, so I'll just forward it to you once I'm not driving," she explained.

Shay must've sensed my wide-eyed stare at her because

she looked to the side as she turned her blinker on to slow and take the exit onto the highway. "What?" she asked, her tone casual.

As if we weren't just chatting about the fact that the sister of the guy I'd tried to dump had just up and bought me a plane ticket to Alaska. And I was so freaked out by what was going on I hadn't even hesitated to jump in the truck and just go.

"What do you mean what?" I countered.

Shay looked back toward the highway, and I saw the curve of a smile on her cheek. "Holly seems to think you and Alex mean a lot to each other. Knowing Holly the way I do, I know she likes you, and I know she thinks Alex will want you there."

"What do you mean?" I asked quickly.

"I mean Holly is kind of a crazy, overprotective sister. There is absolutely no way she would get this ticket if she didn't think Alex wanted to see you and if she didn't like you."

Shay had already assured me after we left the bar that Alex was going to be okay, but I found myself asking yet again, "Are you sure he's going to be okay?"

I'd been feeling half sick and anxious to the point of being shaky ever since she had shown up at the bar to steal me away.

"Here." She lifted her phone out of the cupholder where it was resting in the console. "There's no password. Holly's number is my last phone call. Why don't you call her now?"

Holding the phone in my hand, I resisted the urge to toss it away as if it was on fire. I *did* want to call Holly, but I was afraid, afraid of *so* much.

"What are you afraid of?" Shay gave voice to my own internal question.

I set the phone down, leaning forward and dropping my face into my hands. Taking a deep breath, I let it out, feeling the air filter through my fingers. I finally lifted my head. "I don't know. I haven't even talked to Alex in a few weeks. I broke things off because I thought—" I stopped abruptly, shaking my head. "I don't know what I thought."

Shay kept her eyes ahead as she replied, "You know, Delilah, you've always been intensely independent. I used to envy that about you."

"You did?" I was genuinely shocked because I found it hard to imagine there could be anything about myself to envy.

"I really did. You forget I had a shitty relationship before I got out of it. I used to think if I'd been like you, or maybe Jade—you two remind me of each other—that I never would've ended up there."

Shay was referring to an abusive relationship she'd been in for a few years during and after college. We all knew about it because it was all over the news when her ex got arrested for assault, and then later for a DUI when two passengers were killed in the accident.

"You're pretty strong, if you ask me. Stronger than me. You got through that and look how great things are now," I said.

She cast me a quick look before bringing her eyes immediately back to the road ahead. "Things are good now, but it wasn't easy to get there. Everyone's life is different, the details especially. But I'll say this, Alex seems like a great guy. People who I know and trust vouch for him. I saw you two together. It's obvious you like him. There's no reward without risk. I know that's a cliché, but sometimes clichés become clichés because they're true."

———

I waited in the airport for my flight to be called. I couldn't stop worrying about Alex and obsessively checking my phone. I didn't even know if he'd gotten my text yet.

I laughed to myself. I'd told Shay that I didn't know how I felt. In my panic, I texted him.

I miss you. I'm sorry I haven't called you back.

I'm on my way to Alaska. I'll be there soon.

You better be okay.

I pulled up my phone screen, staring hard at Holly's phone number. Under the stern gaze of Shay, I'd entered it when she dropped me off at the airport, pointing out I would need Holly to tell me how to get to the hospital and probably pick me up.

Noting I still had fifteen minutes before boarding, I took a deep breath and tapped Holly's number to call. It rang only once.

"Delilah! Please tell me you're at the airport," Holly demanded.

"I'm at the airport. Is Alex okay?"

"I told Shay to tell you he was fine. Okay, maybe he's not one hundred percent, but he's going to be fine. One of my best friends was his nurse all night and assured me his numbers were good."

"What happened?"

"We're not really sure. Alex was at the airport doing some maintenance on a plane. Another plane was coming in to land, and there was an explosion in one of the engines as the plane landed. Alex was pulling out the pilot, who probably got knocked out during the landing, when another explosion went off. They think it was the gas tank. We don't know why it exploded yet. We won't know until they do the official investigation and release the findings."

"So what happened to Alex?"

"He saved Fred's life. Fred's a pilot, and he's been around forever. Fred was already unconscious, and then Alex was knocked out with the second explosion. The passengers had gotten out and dragged him and Fred out of the way."

"What are his injuries?" My stomach was churning and churning and churning.

"He had a mild concussion, and he's got ringing intermittently in his ear. He's all scraped up on his back from falling on the pavement. He's going to be sore, but he's going to be okay. They kept him overnight for observation because he was unconscious when he got there. He also was having trouble breathing at first. I think he had a mild case of blast lung." She paused, and then, "Delilah? Are you still there?"

I didn't realize a tear was rolling down my cheek until it hit the corner of my mouth. I swiped it away, sniffling as I replied, "Yeah, I'm here."

"I'm glad you're at the airport. I tried to get you a better flight schedule, but there weren't many options on such short notice. You won't get here until tomorrow evening because of the layovers in Houston and then Seattle tomorrow. I made sure you have a hotel voucher in Houston if you need it tonight. I figured you might want it with a seven-hour layover. There's a hotel right by the airport."

"It's fine. Actually, it's amazing. You didn't have to do this," I said quickly. "It doesn't seem like there are many direct options from here to Alaska."

"I'd say not, and it's faster to fly to Europe from the East Coast than to Alaska," Holly said wryly.

"I know. I'm just glad I'll be there soon."

"Maybe I overstepped, but I—"

I cut in. "You didn't. I want to see him. I'm just not so sure he'll want to see me."

"Oh, he will," Holly said firmly. "I know you broke up with him."

I was glad Holly couldn't see my face because I was so embarrassed. "Holly—" I began

It was her turn to interrupt. "I get it. It's just I can tell you mean a lot to him, so I decided to make fate intervene."

"Are you fate?" I asked between sniffles.

Holly laughed. "Maybe, maybe not. I thought I would nudge things along. The rest is up to you and Alex."

Chapter Thirty-Four

ALEX

The next day - Alaska

"Holly," I practically growled, not even bothering to keep the irritation out of my voice.

"What?" Her voice was all innocence and sweetness. I wasn't fooled. My twin sister was anything but innocent and sweet. She was up to something, but hell if I knew what. I was too tired to figure it out.

"I'm home, and I would like some privacy. Please."

"Just let me stop by and check on you," she insisted.

I heard Nate say something in the background. I could've sworn he said, "Why don't you tell him?"

"What the hell is Nate talking about?"

Holly hung up on me.

"What the hell?" I muttered entirely to myself.

They'd let me escape the hospital late yesterday afternoon. After they ran a battery of tests, I was cleared to go home. I was expected to have some shortness of breath for a few days, but Charlie told me I was good to go. I was supposed to go see her in her office at the end of this week. Between my mother fussing over me since yesterday, in addition to Holly, I was ready to scream. I just wanted to relax, which wasn't easy. My back was sore from the scraping from the asphalt.

I tossed my phone on the coffee table and reached for the remote. After a few minutes, I settled on the background noise of the news because I couldn't find a show I wanted to watch. I looked at my phone again, opening the text from Delilah. I had already sent her a return text when I got my phone back, but that wasn't until today. I'd left it at the airport, and no one knew where the hell it was. Nate had driven me out there, and I'd found it in my bag of tools where I'd tucked it when I started working.

So far, nothing but silence from Delilah in response to my text. I didn't know what she meant about coming to Alaska. I figured that meant she was planning a trip and would let me know when.

Standing, I made my way into the kitchen, ignoring the pain in my back. I opened my refrigerator, only to be reminded I hadn't done any grocery shopping yet this week. I pulled out a bottle of beer and the last two pieces of left-over pizza I'd gotten three days ago.

I was sitting on the couch finishing a slice of pizza when there was a knock on the door. "Come in!" I called, figuring it was Holly and maybe Nate.

The door opened slowly, almost hesitantly, which was my first clue it wasn't Holly. She was more likely to come in with a flourish.

"Alex?"

I stood quickly, and my breath hissed through my teeth when the skin on my back pulled tight.

"Delilah?"

I was crossing the room just as she peered around the door. My heart kicked up a racket in my chest, and my breath seized in my lungs for a moment.

She stepped in and closed the door behind her. "Holly's not coming over, but she dropped me off." Delilah's eyes searched my face.

I closed the distance between us in a few strides and pulled her almost roughly into my arms. Delilah didn't hesitate, stepping close and wrapping her arms carefully around my waist as she tucked her head into the crook of my neck.

"I'm so glad you're okay." Her voice was muffled against my shirt.

I had one arm wrapped around her back and the other cupping the back of her head. I tried to catch my breath, but it wasn't working very well.

Delilah stepped back. "Are you okay?" She peered up at me, her eyes watery with tears. "Holly said you might have trouble with your breathing for a few days."

With my heart racing, I closed my eyes, forcing myself to take a slow, steadying breath.

Delilah placed her hand on my chest over my heart, circling it lightly. When I opened my eyes again, her concerned gaze was trained on my face. "You need to sit down."

I opened my mouth to protest, but then I decided I didn't mind Delilah fussing over me. Not even a little. The relief of having her here was so enormous I couldn't put words to it. My entire body felt full of feeling.

Her hands fluttered over me as she pushed me toward the couch. "How's your back? Do you need a pillow? I don't know how to prop you up without it hurting your back." She looked down at me, her brow furrowed.

"It's fine," I assured her. "It's sore, but it's nothing more than bad scrapes."

She insisted on propping pillows all around me, and then looked at the coffee table where my half empty bottle of beer sat with the pizza box and some napkins thrown in it. "Should I clean up?"

She didn't even give me a chance to reply, whisking away

the pizza box and asking if I needed another beer. When I chuckled and pointed out I still had half of the one there, she pursed her lips. "Wait a sec. Are you even supposed to have beer?"

My girl was nervous, her fingers twitching along her elbows as she wrapped her arms around her waist. I held my hand out, beckoning her. After a moment, she stepped closer. Her palm was clammy in mine, further giving away just how nervous she was. "Come here."

With a little tug from me, Delilah acquiesced, sitting carefully and smoothing her free hand over her thigh. "I'm sorry," she blurted out. "I panicked. I love you."

Oh, well then, I guess we were just going to dive right into the deep end of this. Joy exploded in my chest.

"Thank God," I said as I looked into her tearful eyes. "Because I love you too. We're gonna figure this out. Geography is irrelevant."

Delilah bit her lip, her worried eyes scanning my face. "You didn't have to say that just because I did," she finally said.

"I didn't say it just because you did. I said it because I meant it."

I brushed her hair away from her face, letting my thumb trail down to cup her cheek with my palm. I gave a subtle tug on her hand, trying to pull her across my lap.

Delilah narrowed her eyes. "You're injured."

"Not that bad," I murmured as I succeeded in pulling her onto my lap.

She landed sideways with her breath coming out in a startled gasp. "Alex!"

"Right here, sweetheart." I cupped her nape and pulled her closer.

She relaxed against me as I teased my lips over hers. She murmured something, the words lost in our kiss. I teased my tongue against hers briefly before leaning back.

"What did you say?"

"You're injured," she repeated.

"Not that bad. They wouldn't have discharged me from the hospital if I wasn't okay. Holly would've personally killed someone there if they had," I said with a chuckle.

Delilah's gaze softened, her lips curling in a slow smile. "I'm sure she would have."

As we stared at each other, it felt as if the air around us began to vibrate, humming with that subtle electricity that was ever present when I was near Delilah. My cock swelled, and Delilah's eyes widened.

"I don't really want to talk right now." My words came out husky.

Delilah opened her mouth, most likely to protest, but I didn't give her a chance. I tugged her closer again and devoured her mouth with a kiss.

None of my body's assorted aches and pains mattered. Although she tried to stop me once or twice, she gave in when I told her I just needed her.

I didn't remember how we got our clothes off. I *did* remember Delilah straddling me on the couch, sinking down slowly as she sheathed me in her slick, clenching channel. I felt her ripple around me, her entire body shuddering slightly just before she cried out my name when she came all over my cock.

My release hit me with a sharp, sizzling burst of pleasure. Delilah fell against me, tucking her head into my shoulder. I held her because that was all I wanted. Delilah in my arms. *Exactly* where she was supposed to be.

Chapter Thirty-Five

DELILAH

"How are you?" Janet asked. She had one hand on her hip with a coffee pot held in the other hand.

Alex winced slightly as he leaned back in his chair. My heart winced in response. I'd seen the scrapes in question on his back last night and again this morning. Sure, they were technically scrapes, but they were awful. Holly told me his shirt had torn, likely from the blast when he was thrown back onto the pavement. A cotton T-shirt isn't all that much protection.

Alex smirked. "I'm fine. How are you?"

Janet rolled her eyes and looked at me. "Is he really fine?"

Looking from Janet to Alex and back again, I let out a sigh. "I think it depends on your definition of fine."

Alex grinned again. "I am fine," he protested. "What I need is one of your omelets to make my day start just right."

Janet smiled, dropping her hand from her hip to reach over and squeeze him gently on the shoulder. "Coming right up. What kind?"

"Whatever you want to make me. Just make sure it has bacon."

"Absolutely. Thank you for getting Fred out of that plane. You know how fond I am of him. All of us are fond of him."

Alex gave an easy shrug, nonchalant and all. "I just did what he would've done for me, and I'm glad he's all right. We're going to go up and check on him at the hospital after breakfast."

"Holly told me it looks like he's lost his hearing in one ear. How about you?" Janet asked.

"I think my hearing's going to be fine. The ringing is almost gone this morning. The hearing specialist told me it might be a few days, but that everything was still in working order."

"And your lungs?" Janet prompted.

"I'm breathing."

Janet rolled her eyes just as someone called her name from the counter. She glanced at me. "Anything for breakfast for you?"

"I'll take a bagel with your smoked salmon cream cheese."

"Both of your orders will be out shortly." Janet hurried off.

Looking across the table at Alex, I said, "Promise me you'll be honest about how your breathing feels."

Alex narrowed his eyes. "I promise. How long will you be here?" he asked, quickly changing the subject.

"Holly got me an open-ended round-trip ticket, which was really nice of her. I promised her I'd pay her back. I get to pick my return date. Fortunately, I remembered to pack my laptop, so I can do classes while I'm here. I need to call work to figure out how long they can make do without me. I'd like to stay for at least two weeks."

Alex's chocolate eyes searched mine. "You can stay as long as you'd like. I know you'll need to go home, but maybe at some point while you're here, we could talk about possibilities."

"I'd love that," I said. I still felt a little anxious, not quite sure how to embrace this positive possibility in my world. Against all odds, I had faith Alex and I would figure it out.

Surprisingly, I truly did have faith. Although I had to remind myself of that often, I stayed the two weeks and loved every minute of it. I even went with Alex to his second follow-up appointment with Charlie a few days before I was scheduled to return to Stolen Hearts Valley.

Looking around the small office, I sat on a chair beside him. It was like most doctors' offices, painted in neutral colors with soothing watercolors hanging on the walls, in the midst of plenty of health informational posters.

"I think you'll like Charlie," Alex commented from my side.

"All I want to know is if your lungs are back to one hundred percent."

"My hearing has to be." Alex smirked. "I definitely heard you this morning."

My cheeks got hot. I might have been a little loud this morning. "It's all your fault," I muttered, nudging him with my elbow. "Also, behave. We're at the doctor's office."

Alex gave me an incredulous look before shaking his head. "We're in this room alone. Charlie's not even here yet."

"Yeah, but she—" I began, just as the door opened, and a woman stepped in.

Charlie was beautiful. She had dark hair pulled back in a ponytail with streaks of pink and purple visible. She was dressed in the typical doctor's uniform with a white coat over her slacks. Her warm gray gaze looked from Alex to me as a smile teased at the corners of her mouth. "Hi there," she said with a brisk nod.

Apparently, this was not a town that stood on ceremony as far as insisting on the title of doctor.

"Nice to meet you," I said, standing and holding out my hand. "I'm Delilah."

"Charlie Franklin," she replied with a firm handshake. "Great to meet you. I've heard good things about you."

"You've heard about me?" I squeaked as I sat down quickly, clasping my hands together over my knees.

"Oh, yes. Rachel's my medical assistant. She told me she thinks you should be my nursing intern next year."

Charlie's tone was casual and relaxed, but her comment suddenly had me tense. I did want to figure out what Alex and I were going to do to be able to be together full-time, yet every time I was standing on the edge of a decision, I felt as if I were about to step off a cliff. My habits of not needing anyone and taking care of myself were so deeply ingrained, it was hard for me to push myself beyond them.

When Charlie glanced at me as she turned to wheel a stool with a mounted laptop attached to the side, I simply smiled, and said, "Oh, you're the doctor Rachel works with."

Charlie nodded as she clicked a few keys on the keyboard. "Take all the time you need to decide, but we do take an intern every year. It's definitely a possibility if you're interested. But that's not why you're here today." Her eyes flicked to Alex.

He suddenly looked a little uncomfortable, shifting his shoulders. I'd discovered he was a rather typical man when it came to his health. I generally loathed stereotypes, but sometimes, they fit. Alex hated feeling weak, and he hated going to the doctor. Even when he professed that he even liked his doctor.

"How are those scrapes healing?" Charlie asked.

Alex stood and moved to take his shirt off. Charlie held a hand up. "I don't actually need to see them. They looked well on their way to healing last week. Unless you want me to check them?"

Alex's arms fell back to his sides, and he shrugged. "I don't think so. They itch like hell, so I figure that's a good sign. Right?"

"Absolutely. It means they're healing. I need you to sit here," she said, patting the examination table. "I want to listen to your lungs."

The paper crinkled as Alex shifted his hips onto the table. When I glanced up and saw the subtle uncertainty and vulnerability flickering in his eyes, my heart squeezed.

Charlie tapped a few keys on the keyboard and then moved to stand beside the table. She rested a stethoscope on his back, instructing him through several rounds of deep breathing as she checked both sides. After she removed the earpieces, she smiled. "Your lungs sound great, so you're all set. I don't need to see you again. I'm assuming you've already checked in with the hearing specialist?"

"Oh, yeah. This one is still a tiny bit off," he explained, tugging on his left earlobe, "but she said it should resolve because I can hear noises at all volumes. Explosions are loud, in case you didn't know."

Charlie laughed as she turned and checked on her computer again, entering a few things on the keyboard. "Before you go, make sure to schedule your next physical. I'm not seeing it in your appointment calendar."

Alex looked a little sheepish, so I piped up, "I'll make sure he does it."

"Don't gang up on me," he said when Charlie flashed me a knowing grin.

"I'm not ganging up on you. You need to get your annual physical."

As we were leaving, Charlie called, "Think about that internship, Delilah."

Turning back in the hallway, I nodded. "I will. Really."

Chapter Thirty-Six

ALEX

Autumn

"What have you and Delilah decided?" my sister asked, tightening her lips in a line and lasering me with her eyes. That was Holly's way of trying to look bossy.

"We've decided we're not going to decide until Delilah's father passes."

I didn't add that the uncertainty of that timeline was difficult for me. I was impatient, and I felt a little guilty for feeling impatient. I completely understood Delilah wanting to wait since her father's cancer was terminal, but I missed her. We'd settled into a cycle of seeing each other roughly every other month with lots and lots of video calls between and daily texts, of course.

It didn't change that I missed her to the point that my heart ached sometimes.

"What's his status?" Holly asked, her bossy tone fading.

I lifted my hands and let them fall. "We're not sure. He was diagnosed last winter before she went to Diamond

Creek. At the time, they only gave him four to six months. Obviously, he's overshot that."

"What kind of cancer is it? I know you told me, but I can't remember."

"Colon cancer."

Holly's lips twisted to the side. "That sucks. I bet it's hard on her just waiting, and she probably also wants him to live longer. It's a terrible place for families to be."

Knowing how thoroughly private Delilah was, I hadn't shared the details about her not-so-great childhood with anyone else. I figured that was her story to tell if she ever wanted to tell it. She and her mother seemed to be mending fences, so I thought that was good. She'd also assured me she and her father had a few conversations that helped. Apparently, he slept almost all the time now.

"Have you two even talked about what the plan might be?" Holly asked, her words careful, which was so unusual for her that I almost laughed.

We were having coffee at Firehouse Café. I looked over at Nate. His lips twitched with a smile, and I knew he'd noticed her caution. He knew Holly as well as I did, probably even better now.

"I think she's going to come here, but I don't want to push her to make anything final, not right now. It just doesn't feel right."

"Just wait," Nate chimed in. "Long-distance relationships are hard enough. Throw in a parent who's sick and dying, and four thousand miles or so between you, and you don't wanna add to the pressure."

"What he said," I replied before draining my coffee.

Over the next few weeks, I found my communication with Delilah was more sporadic. That worried me. She was busy enough as it was without any actual complications getting in the way.

Late one night, I got a text from Shay. "Call me."

Well, that was weird. Shay had been instrumental in

getting Delilah out here after my accident, but it's not like we chatted or texted often.

I called her immediately. "What's up?" I asked the moment she answered.

"Hey, you have my number in your phone, Alex. I feel special," she teased.

"You texted," I replied.

"I did." Shay paused to clear her throat. "Delilah's father passed away today. I happened to see her at the gas station, and she doesn't look good. I didn't know if she'd called to let you know."

I silently swore.

As if Shay could read my mind, she said softly, "You know how private she is, Alex. She's not used to leaning on anyone."

"I do. I'm coming there. I'll catch the first flight I can. Don't tell her."

"Do you need a ride?" Shay asked swiftly.

"No, but thanks. I'll just rent a car at the airport."

Chapter Thirty-Seven

DELILAH

I just felt strange. That was the only way I could describe how I felt after my father finally died. Grieving someone when they're still alive and you knew they wouldn't ultimately survive was exhausting.

My emotional state felt gray, and I was tired and irritable on top of it. I also felt guilty because I hadn't called Alex yet. My father had only died the night before. I'd spent the night with my mother, and it hadn't felt right to call him then.

Now, it was the following afternoon, and I was at the funeral home helping to make plans. I'd gotten myself psyched out. I needed to call him and let him know what happened.

"Do you know if your mother would like a casket? Or are you planning to have him cremated?" the gracious funeral director asked.

This man had the absolute perfect demeanor for his job. He was calm and soothing. I imagined I could tell him anything, and he would simply nod and smile gently at me.

The problem was I didn't know what my mother wanted. Although my mother and I'd been talking a lot more than

usual lately, she hadn't said a thing to me about funeral planning. When I'd asked her earlier, she said she didn't know.
Apparently, there was no plan.

"Can you tell me what you recommend for a family who
doesn't have a plan?"

My pleasant funeral director didn't miss a beat. "The
biggest choice is whether you'd like a casket or cremation. If
you don't have a preference, I usually recommend cremation.
If only because it's more affordable. The internment of ashes
in a permanent location allows you to visit just as one would
if you'd chosen a casket burial."

"Okay, let's do that."

The next thing I knew, I was in his office signing paperwork and texting my mother with various questions, to
which she kept replying, "Whatever you think."

I knew grief made people weird, but this was annoying. I
had a headache, and I was waiting for the funeral director to
return to his office with several urns for me to choose from.
A sound from the doorway drew my attention. Alex stood
there. His eyes swept over me, and he stepped hesitantly in
my direction.

I leaped out of my chair and basically threw myself in his
arms, bursting into tears the moment he caught me in his
strong embrace. I heard the rumble of his voice murmuring
something as I pressed my cheek against his chest and hung
onto him. His hand moved up and down my back in
soothing passes. I hiccupped and finally lifted my head, sniffling when I saw his concerned dark eyes.

"I'm kind of a mess. I meant to call you and..." I lifted a
hand, flailing it in the air.

"You don't have to explain. Your dad died. Shay texted
me late last night, so I got on a plane. There are no rules
about this when somebody dies. It's more important for you
to be there for your mom than to worry about calling me."

The relief that washed through me was so profound my
knees almost gave out. At that moment, the funeral director

reappeared with a large box in his hands. Unflappable as he had already demonstrated himself to be, he glanced back and forth between us. "Shall I give you two a moment?"

"If you don't mind," I replied

He bowed his head and turned away, closing the door behind him. The ridiculousness of my reunion with my boyfriend at a funeral parlor in the director's office struck me, and I started giggling. Those giggles turned into laughter, and I was crying by the time I could catch my breath. Alex stepped away and fetched a box of tissues conveniently located right on the corner of the desk. I imagined there were tissues practically everywhere in this building.

"Are you okay?"

As I felt the low rumble of his voice reverberate through my body, I could finally take a deep breath. The tightness and coldness in my chest that I'd been carrying for what felt like weeks now as my father slowly slid away eased.

"I am. You didn't have to—"

Alex's look stopped me. "There are no have to's. I wanted to be here. Now, how can I help?"

Because apparently, I'd turned into a watering pot, I burst into tears again.

Chapter Thirty-Eight

ALEX

"Are you sure?" Delilah asked.

I looked over at her. We were at her apartment, sitting on her couch. We'd done a few other errands and then gotten takeout pizza after the meeting at the funeral home. Delilah's calves were resting across my lap as she leaned into the corner of the couch. She looked tired, her eyes a little red from crying, and what seemed to be a permanent furrow between her brows, at least this afternoon.

"Of course I'm sure. I didn't fly all the way out here just to turn around and leave. I'll stay as long as you'd like."

"As long as I'd like? Well, in that case..." she began with a smile. It was a tired smile, but nonetheless, I was glad to see she could tease.

I lightly squeezed one of her feet. It was warm through the cotton of her socks. She let out a sigh as she leaned her head back. "That feels good."

I started massaging her feet, alternating between them. After we'd gotten to her place this evening, she'd turned the television on to a home and garden show. That seemed to be her preferred background noise.

She was quiet for a few minutes and then looked toward me, catching my eyes immediately. "I've been thinking." After that loaded start, she paused.

"About what?" I prompted.

"Us."

A sense of trepidation slid through me. We'd been saying we'd figure things out after her father passed. I just didn't expect her to want to have that conversation this very second.

I took a breath and nodded. "What about us?"

"I'm going to move to Alaska."

"Delilah, you don't have to—"

She shook her head quickly. "I know I don't have to decide now if that's where you were going. It's what I want. I've even talked to my mom about it. She's planning on staying here, but she'll come out and visit several times a year. She would be the only thing holding me here, and I want to look to the future, not the past."

My heart was thudding so fast for a moment that my breath was locked in my chest. After a few beats, I managed to let it out in a gust and tugged her a little closer to me. "Are you sure this is what you want?"

"Absolutely."

"What's the future for you?"

"I don't know all the details, but I know it includes us together in one place."

"You know I'd come here for you, right? I've been thinking about it."

Delilah nodded as she lifted a hand, smoothing one of my brows with her fingertip. "I know you've been trying not to bring it up because of what's been going on with my dad, and I appreciate that. But I love you, and I want to be with you. There's a lot more to the life you have in Alaska than what I have here, and I love it there. That summer after we met at camp, all I could think about was how it would be so cool to live there. Now, I can."

"Are you sure you want to make this decision now?"

I almost couldn't believe Delilah was already pushing ahead. I'd been trying so hard not to pressure her.

Her lips curled in a slow smile. "Yes, Alex. I'm sure. It's not like I haven't had time to think about it. The decision is pretty easy. It'll be harder to decide where I do my internship, although I'm leaning toward Charlie's office."

"I love you," I murmured as I pulled her onto my lap and held her close.

EPILOGUE
Delilah

December

I looked out the plane's window at the snow-covered Kenai Mountains, the peaks dark against the bright blue winter sky. As the plane lowered, I could see the single highway winding down the Kenai Peninsula.

My pulse kicked up a notch not much later as the plane landed with a little rumble and a bump. I couldn't wait to see Alex. Minutes later, I saw him waiting for me, his brown hair shaggy and a shadow of stubble visible on his strong, square jaw.

I wasn't much for being romantic. Although I loved Alex so much, this past year had been hard because I'd missed him too damn much. Every minute we found together felt like a mirage, so I said goodbye to Stolen Hearts Valley when I boarded this plane. I would miss my friends dearly, but the call of a fresh start beckoned me.

The moment I saw him, I began running, dropping my bag as he swung me into his arms. Tears pressed hot at the backs of my eyes as joy nearly burst my heart out of my chest. His strong arms squeezed me tightly, and I pressed kisses along his neck before leaning back to pepper his face with more. "I missed you!" I exclaimed.

"I don't know if you could've missed me as much as I missed you. It's been a long four weeks," he murmured, brushing my tangled hair away from my face before going still, his espresso gaze holding mine and conveying far more than words ever could. He brushed a tear away as it rolled down my cheek. "Now what are you crying for?" He brought his lips to mine for a quick kiss before pulling back and waiting for my answer.

"I'm just happy, so happy it almost hurts."

A smile stretched from one corner of his mouth to the other. "I am *so* fucking glad you're here."

"Delilah!" a voice called. Though Alex eased me to the ground, he kept one arm firmly around me. Glancing over my shoulder, I saw Holly waving. Nate cracked a smile and leaned over to say something in her ear.

"You have a welcoming committee," Alex said. He stepped away to pick up my bag, immediately reaching for my hand again with his free hand. "Anything to pick up in baggage claim?"

I shook my head, taking a deep breath and letting it out with a slow sigh. The relief I felt at finally being here mingled with immense joy, and a sense of coming home echoed through my body. "I shipped almost everything. It should get here in a couple of days," I replied.

Hours later, I stepped out into a cold, snowy night on the deck outside our room. A Christmas tree glittered in the dark behind the ski lodge. I'd taken Marley up on the free two weeks after last year's snafu. Alex stopped in front of me, turning and looking back. "Merry Christmas," he said simply.

With a little tug on my hand, he reeled me close. I bumped into him, savoring his warmth and strength as he slid his arms around my waist. "I promise you're gonna love it in Alaska," he murmured.

"I'm not worried." Because I wasn't. "We never did decide if we were doing Christmas presents." I angled my head back to look into his eyes, the snow cool where it landed on my cheeks as it fell softly from the sky.

"You're my Christmas present," he murmured right before bringing his lips to mine.

———

Thank you for reading That Snowy Night - I hope you loved Delilah & Alex's story!

This Crazy Love kicks off the Swoon Series - small town southern romance with enough heat to melt you. I promise you this series has plenty of alpha men with hearts of gold & sassy women who bring them to their knees!

Jackson & Shay's story is epic - swoon-worthy & intensely emotional. Jackson just happens to be Shay's brother's best friend. He's also *seriously* easy on the eyes. Shay has a past, the kind of past she would most definitely like to forget. Past or not, Jackson is about to rock her world. Don't miss their story!

Keep reading for a sneak peek!

Be sure to sign up for my newsletter for the latest news, teasers & more! Click here to sign up: http://jhcroixauthor.com/subscribe/

EXCERPT: THIS CRAZY LOVE

Shay

I climbed out of my car, wincing slightly as the door squeaked when I tried to shut it. With a little extra push, it closed all the way. My car was a bit like me. It was hanging in there, but it was rough around the edges. I was rather attached to it. In fact, lately, I felt more kindly toward my car than myself.

Before my thoughts meandered too far down that path—a well-worn rut of recrimination and regret—my attention was snagged by a small horse galloping across the pasture in front of me. The horse was almost black with three white feet, as if it were missing a sock.

The horse angled to the side, just enough for me to see its tail flick behind it and notice it was a male. He kicked his back feet up in the air and turned to face the fence again. A white star stood out in the center of his forehead.

I was so absorbed in watching, I didn't quite notice what he was about to do until he came sailing over the fence in a beautiful jump, the kind that would've gotten him a ribbon in a show. Except we weren't in a show, and he'd just jumped out of the pasture. The horse came running straight for me, skidding to a stop before snorting and pawing at the ground.

Just as I was about to reach out, he spun around and dashed off again, kicking dirt in my face.

"Mischief!" a voice called.

Sputtering, I dragged my sleeve across my face. Looking ahead, I saw a man in the distance. A loud whistle followed his call. I wondered if that was Jackson Stone. I wasn't close enough to see from here. Whoever it was, he walked with an easy strength and grace along the fence line.

Taking a deep breath, I glanced around. I'd left before dawn this morning. A few hours of driving got me here just as the sun was rising behind the mountains. The famous blue haze over the Blue Ridge Mountains was shot through with gold from the sun's early rays.

My gaze made its way back to the horse I presumed to be Mischief. He slowed to a trot as the man approached him and then came to a stop, docilely lowering his head as the man slipped a halter on him. I watched as they turned toward me again. It was a minute or so before they reached me, but I recognized Jackson once he was close enough.

I once had a bit of a crush on Jackson, years back. With his shaggy brown curls and his piercing blue eyes, it was fair to say I was not the only girl who had a crush on him. I didn't think it was quite possible, but when he stopped in front of me, he was somehow more handsome than he had been before.

He wore scuffed leather boots with jeans, and a black T-shirt that didn't do much of anything to obscure the fact that he had a body to die for, all muscle and hard planes.

Stopping in front of me, his mouth curled into a slow smile. "How's it going, Shay?"

"Aside from getting dirt kicked in my face, I'm fine," I said with a laugh.

Jackson's smile turned sheepish with a shrug. "Sorry 'bout that. Mischief lives up to his name." He glanced to the horse in question, giving him an affectionate rub under his chin. "Mischief, this is Shay, and she's a friend. So, be nice. He doesn't listen too well," he added with a glance to me.

As if he understood, and to prove Jackson wrong, Mischief lifted his nose, gently nudging my shoulder with it. Despite teasing, I didn't really care about getting dirt kicked in my face. Dirt was the least of my worries. I lifted a hand and scratched between Mischief's ears, rewarded when he lowered his head and rubbed against my shoulder again.

When I looked back to Jackson, his blue gaze had darkened. A prickle ran up my spine, and I wondered if coming here was the smartest move. Problem was, it was my *only* move. I didn't have any other good options.

I forced a smile and replied, "Well, he listens to you."

A grin stretched across Jackson's face, and my belly executed a little flip. Oh my.

"He listens when he wants and that's about it. Let me get him back in the pasture, and I'll take you inside."

I watched as Jackson strolled across the parking area toward the fence Mischief had just cleared in an easy jump, as if it was nothing more than a minor nuisance. Opening the gate, Jackson slipped his halter off and patted him on the rump as Mischief flicked his tail before trotting off to join a cluster of horses in the far corner of the pasture.

"Need help carrying anything inside?" Jackson asked, as he stopped beside me.

His eyes traveled to my beat-up little hatchback. If he had an opinion about it, he stayed quiet. Once upon a time —which felt like forever ago at this point—I had a pretty good life.

I certainly had a car in better shape, and enough money to get by. Now, I didn't want to tell anyone how much I needed this place to stay right now. I had *maybe* fifty bucks left in my bank account. My little car was one of the few things that had seen me through both good and bad and was still chugging along, albeit a little banged up.

I watched Jackson's gaze coast over my car, hoping he didn't wonder about the dent just underneath the window in the driver's side door. A fist had left that behind. I didn't have the money to fix it and had learned insurance didn't cover people punching your car.

"Shay?" Jackson asked, his voice nudging me out of this ditch on memory lane, where I tended to get trapped.

"Oh right. I just have two bags," I replied quickly, finally springing into motion and striding over to my car.

Jackson insisted on carrying one of the bags, his fingers brushing mine and sending a hot little zing up my arm. I hadn't seen Jackson in five long years, but I'd never forgotten how handsome he was. Dear God, the man was swoon-worthy and then some. Yet, I didn't recall reacting this way to him before, even if I'd crushed on him a little when I was younger and shared a single, wild kiss one night.

That zing startled me. I had written off desire, figuring my life would be better off without it. I also figured I was pretty much ruined for it. That's what a few years of bad sex tangled up with fear could do. It made me question everything about desire and my own judgment.

As I looked ahead to the farmhouse, I reminded myself, rather sternly, I needed this to work out. I needed a place to regroup, and this was it. Even *thinking* about the sudden, confusing attraction to my brother's best friend was a bad idea.

JACKSON

Shay had a mere two bags with her. "I can get one," she said, her tone a little testy when I moved to take both bags. Shay had always liked to do things for herself, so I let it go and turned with the one I already had in hand.

Moments later, we were inside the house. I led her through the sprawling farmhouse kitchen, down the hall, and up the stairs, going straight to the bedroom Ash had determined would be Shay's.

After our father passed away a few years ago, my sister and I inherited the family farm. Years back, it had been a working farm for generations of our family. In the last decade or so before our father passed away, he had wound down the farming part of it, and dedicated his time to his horses and creating an animal rescue sanctuary. Before our mother died, he promised her someday he'd make the farm into a rescue.

Our father's death brought me home. In addition to the rescue program, we ran a small veterinary clinic, seeing as I had my license, but I hadn't put it to much use while I'd been overseas in the military. We'd also renovated two of the massive old barns into a high-end adventure lodge. We hosted a variety of guests throughout the year.

Ash was only here occasionally of late and was out of town now. She was one hundred percent on board with having Shay come stay here, so she made all the decisions about which room and so on.

Stopping by the door to the guestroom in question, I glanced back to Shay. "Right in here," I said, pausing once I stepped inside and set her bag on the floor in front of the dresser.

When I looked over at Shay again, my breath was nearly knocked out of me. The early morning sunlight hadn't done her justice. If I thought she was beautiful before, she was arresting now. Her dark blonde hair fell loosely around her shoulders. Her green eyes held mine as she looked at me, a hint of defiance entering her gaze.

Shay was on the short side and all curves. She wore fitted jeans and cowboy boots paired with a blouse. Even with her loose blouse, her breasts filled it, curves rising above the rounded neckline. Her lips were full and plump. She arched a brow as I looked at her.

"What?" she demanded.

I gave my head a little shake. "Not a thing. Ash will be thrilled to know you're here. You must've left early. Come on downstairs when you're ready. I'll take a quick shower and then I can show you around."

I walked through the door, trying to ignore the sizzle of electricity in the air when I passed by her. It wasn't until I caught her gaze out of the corner of my eye, and saw the vulnerability under the defiance, that I remembered all the reasons why she was here.

"I'll be down in a little bit. I just want to unpack," she said.

I'd been up for hours and on my back in the dirt, changing the oil on one of the trucks. I needed a shower to clear my head as much as to get clean. I wondered if Shay was too close to my bedroom as I stepped through the doorway at an angle across the hallway. That was a problem for another day.

———

Available now - free on on all retailers!
This Crazy Love

If you love swoon-worthy, small town romance, take a visit to Diamond Creek, Alaska in my Last Frontier Lodge Series. A sexy, alpha SEAL meets his match with a brainy heroine in Take Me Home. It's FREE on all retailers! Don't miss Gage & Marley's story!

Go here to sign up for information on new releases: http://jhcroixauthor.com/subscribe/

FIND MY BOOKS

Thank you for reading That Snowy Night! I hope you enjoyed the story. If so, you can help other readers find my books in a variety of ways.

1) Write a review!
2) Sign up for my newsletter, so you can receive information about upcoming new releases & receive a FREE copy of one of my books: http://jhcroixauthor.com/subscribe/
3) Like and follow my Amazon Author page at https://amazon.com/author/jhcroix
4) Follow me on Bookbub at https://www.bookbub.com/authors/j-h-croix
5) Follow me on Instagram at https://www.instagram.com/jhcroix/
6) Like my Facebook page at https://www.facebook.com/jhcroix

Swoon Series

This Crazy Love

Wait For Me

Break My Fall

Truly Madly Mine

Still Go Crazy

If We Dare

Steal My Heart

Dare With Me Series

Crash Into You

Evers & Afters - coming February 2021!

Come To Me - coming April 2021!

Into The Fire Series

Burn For Me

Slow Burn

Burn So Bad

Hot Mess

Burn So Good

Sweet Fire

Play With Fire

Melt With You

Burn For You

Crash & Burn

That Snowy Night

Brit Boys Sports Romance

The Play

Big Win

Out Of Bounds

Play Me

Naughty Wish

Diamond Creek Alaska Novels

When Love Comes

Follow Love

Love Unbroken

Love Untamed

Tumble Into Love

Christmas Nights
Last Frontier Lodge Novels
Take Me Home
Love at Last
Just This Once
Falling Fast
Stay With Me
When We Fall
Hold Me Close
Crazy For You
Just Us
Catamount Lion Shifters
Protected Mate
Chosen Mate
Fated Mate
Destined Mate
A Catamount Christmas
The Lion Within
Lion Lost & Found